STS

山田社

U0080309

STS

山田社

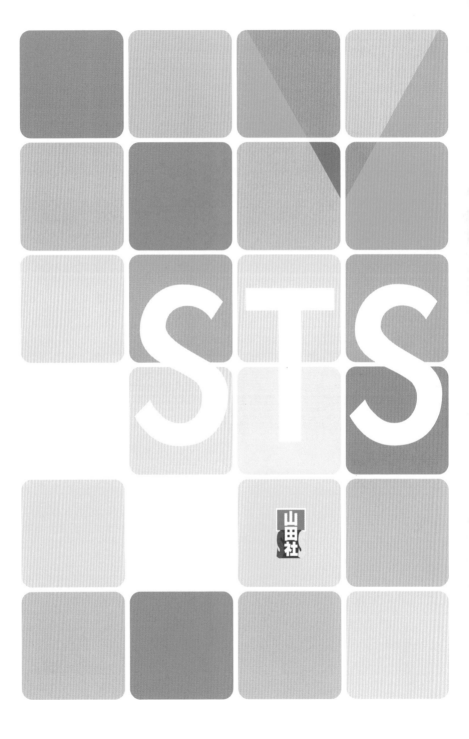

短短的，容易記住的句子，就可以跟老外聊得超過癮！

美國人都這樣
短短說英語

里昂 著

Is this for sale?

You did it!

That's wonderful!

Really?

You finally did it.

Unbelievable!

山田社
Shan Tian She

preface 前言

想學英語，就從隨意閒聊的會話開始吧！

用短短句「輕聊天」，

用自己的嘴巴，流利的說出英語，是一件很酷的事喔！

本書選材：

　　輕鬆一點，感覺像在街頭巷尾聊天談話，內容：興趣、美食、電影、朋友、運動、文化…，天南地北、自由發揮，什麼開心聊什麼。

本書告訴你這樣聊，自然達到流利的境界：

★美國人怎麼描述一件事，你也跟著這麼說。

★學美國人每天都會使用各種慣用說法，說習慣了，

　人家還以為你是美國人。

★自己的生活大小事英語怎麼說呢？就是要讓自己跟

　英語連結起來。

★要活用英語，就要用英語來發問跟討論，刺激自己

　的思考，讓英語活起來。

★別想得太複雜！短短的，容易記住的句子，就可以跟老外聊得超過癮！

本書文法：

對文法沒有太吹毛求疵，就是要讓你解放一下，只要簡單句，短短句，重要的是開口說就對啦！

本書光碟：

想要說得溜，就是要模仿，而且是模仿標準的英語。可以試著模仿光碟中專業美籍老師的發音及腔調。只要不斷地重複，最愛記憶的大腦，就會幫你發揮驚人的效果，多難搞的語言都難不倒你。

用「日曬機」可以很快的曬出一身漂亮的古銅色皮膚，用《美國人都這樣短短說英語》可以讓你隨心所欲溜英語，晚上睡覺都偷笑！

content
目錄

Chapter 1★ 聊聊天簡單到不行

Chapter 2★ 坐車逛街簡單到不行

Chapter 3★ 拜訪朋友簡單到不行

Chapter 4★ 生活旅遊簡單到不行

content
目錄

Chapter 5 ★ 找話題簡單到不行

Chapter 6 ★ 緊急應變 也簡單到不行

Chapter 1

聊聊天簡單到不行

●超好用對話

A：Hi, Mary.

B：Hi, Tom. How is everything?

A：Pretty good. How about you?

B：Well, busy, but fine.

A：Take care of yourself, OK?

中譯

A：嗨，瑪麗。
B：嗨，湯姆。一切都還好嗎？
A：還不賴，妳呢？
B：這個嘛，忙，不過還好。
A：要照顧好自己，好嗎？

精選單字

Hi	everything	good	fine
嗨	每件事，所有事物	好的	很好
How	pretty	busy	take care
如何，怎樣	頗，相當	忙碌的	照顧

1 超好用句型

1 ■ Good <u>morning</u>!
呈安！

Good evening, sir.
■ 晚安！先生。

Good luck!
■ 祝你好運！

替換看看

afternoon	evening	night
下午	傍晚，晚上	晚上
morning	day	to see you
早上	（一）天；白天	見到你

2 ■ How is <u>everything</u>?
一切都還好嗎？

How is Mary?
■ 瑪莉還好嗎？

How is it going?
■ （近況）還好嗎？

替換看看

it going	your family	work
近況	你家人	工作
your wife	school	the new teacher
尊夫人	學校	新老師

★打開話題的好句子

■1 我要這樣說 1-3

- **Good morning!**

  早安！

- **How are you today?**

  你今天好嗎？

- **How is your family?**

  你家人好嗎？

- **How is everything?**

  一切都還好嗎？

- **What's up?**

  怎麼樣呢？

■2 你要那樣說

- **I'm fine, thank you.**

  我很好，謝謝你！

- **Not bad. How about you?**

  還不錯，你呢？

- **I'm great! Thank you!**

  我很好！謝謝你！

- **So far, so good.**

  目前為止，都還好！

- **Nice day, isn't it?**

  天氣不錯吧！

UNIT 2 ★ 叫我小李就好了

 1-4

●超好用對話

A：Hi! My name is Jane.

B：Nice to meet you, Jane. I'm Linda.

A：Nice to meet you, too.

B：Where are you from?

A：I am from Taiwan.

中譯

A：嗨！我的名字是珍。
B：很高興認識妳，珍。我是琳達。
A：我也很高興認識妳。
B：妳是哪裡人？
A：我是台灣來的。

my 我的	nice 很好的	where 哪裡	from 來自
name 名字	too 也	meet 遇見，碰面	Taiwan 台灣

1 超好用句型

1 ■ My name is <u>John Jones</u>.
我的名字是<u>約翰瓊斯</u>。

My name is Ian.
■ 我的名字是伊恩。

My name is Tom.
■ 我的名字是湯姆。

替換看看

Meiling Chen	Ming Wu	Keiko Suzuki
陳美玲	吳明	鈴木惠子
David Shultz	Denzel Washington	James Bond
大衛舒茲	丹佐華盛頓	詹姆士龐德

2 ■ I'm from <u>Canada</u>.
我來自<u>加拿大</u>。

She is from Australia.
■ 她來自澳洲。

Her family is from Europe.
■ 她的家族是從歐洲來的。

替換看看

Taiwan	China	the U.S.A
台灣	中國	美國
Japan	Canada	Korea
日本	加拿大	韓國

★打開話題的好句子

1 我要這樣說

 1-6

- **Excuse me. May I talk to you?**

  不好意思，我可以跟你說話嗎？

- **May I introduce myself?**

  可以讓我自我介紹一下嗎？

- **My name is George.**

  我的名字是喬治。

- **I'm from Canada.**

  我來自加拿大。

- **I'm a student.**

  我是個學生。

2 你要那樣說

- **I'm 20 years old.**

  我20歲。

- **I'm a Libra.**

  我是天秤座。

- **I live in Taipei.**

  我住在台北。

- **I live with my family.**

  我跟家人住。

- **I work for a big company.**

  我在一家大公司上班。

1-7

●超好用對話

A：Tom, this is my wife, Mary.

B：Hello, Mary. Nice to meet you.

C：Hi, Tom! I am glad to meet you, too.

A：Tom's a lawyer.

C：I know. Tom, he has told me a lot about you.

■中譯

A：湯姆，這是我太太瑪麗。
B：嗨！瑪麗，很高興認識妳。
C：嗨，湯姆！我也很高興認識你。
A：湯姆是律師。
C：我知道。湯姆，他跟我說了好多你的事情呢！

精選單字

| wife 妻子 | glad 開心 | know 知道 | a lot 很多 |
| hello 哈囉 | lawyer 律師 | told 告訴 (tell 的過去式) | about 關於 |

1 ■ This is my <u>wife</u>.
這位是我太太。

This is my book.
■ 這是我的書。

This is my bike.
■ 這是我的腳踏車。

替換看看

mother	wife
媽媽	妻子

husband	uncle	aunt	cousin	niece
丈夫	叔叔、舅舅	姨媽、姑姑	表兄弟姐妹	姪女、外甥女
nephew	son	daughter	boyfriend	fiancé
姪子、外甥	兒子	女兒	男朋友	未婚夫（妻）

2 ■ My father is a/an <u>journalist</u>.
我父親是一位記者。

That is a hotel.
■ 那是一家飯店。

This is a new mobile phone.
■ 這是支新的手機。

替換看看

doctor
醫生

nurse	businessperson	writer	reporter	student
護士	商人	作家	記者	學生
fashion designer	teacher	police officer	lawyer	
服裝設計師	老師	警察	律師	

★打開話題的好句子

■1 我要這樣說

 1-9

- Let me introduce you to my son, John.

  讓我來跟你介紹一下,這是我兒子約翰。

- This is Mary.

  這是瑪莉。

- Jeff, this is Ana. Ana, this is Jeff.

  傑夫,這位是安娜。安娜,這位是傑夫。

- Nice to meet you.

  很高興認識你。

- I am Frank. It's so nice to meet you.

  我是法蘭克,真的很高興認識你。

■2 你要那樣說

- He is from Chicago.

  他來自芝加哥。

- Have you met already?

  你們見過面了嗎?

- I'd like to meet your wife.

  我很高興能見到您夫人。

- I think you'll be good friends.

  我覺得你們可以成為好朋友。

- We often talk to each other.

  我們經常聊天。

UNIT 4 ★ 下回見啦

1-10

●超好用對話

A：I have to go now.

B：Okay, Say hello to your family for me.

A：I sure will. See you next time.

B：Good luck!

中譯

A：我現在得走了。
B：好的！請代我向你家人問好。
A：我會的。下回見。
B：祝你好運！

have to 必須	now 現在	family 家人	see 看見
go 走	say 說	sure 肯定，必定	luck 運氣

1 超好用句型

1 ■ See you <u>tomorrow</u>.
明天見。

See you there.
■ 那裡見。

See you around.
■ 隨後見。

替換看看

next Monday	next year	later
下星期一	明年	晚點
next time	soon	again
下一次	很快	再次

2 ■ Have a <u>nice weekend</u>!
祝你有個美好的週末！

Have a wonderful time.
■ 祝你玩得愉快。

Have a great date.
■ 祝你有個美好的約會。

替換看看

nice flight	nice trip	nice voyage
愉快的飛行	愉快的旅途	愉快的航行
wonderful vacation	pleasant flight	good day
美好的假期	愉快的飛航	美好的一天

★打開話題的好句子

▊1 我要這樣說

 1-12

■ How have you been?

最近可好？

■ I've been fine, thank you. And you?

我很好。謝謝你！你呢？

■ I've been fine, too. Thank you.

我也很好。謝謝你！

■ What a surprise to see you!

能跟你碰面真叫人意外啊！

■ Good bye!

再見！

▊2 你要那樣說

■ Take care!

路上小心！

■ Have a nice weekend!

祝你有個快樂的週末！

■ Good luck.

祝你好運！

■ Bye-bye. Don't work too hard.

再見！工作不要太辛苦了。

■ Say hello to your wife for me.

請代我向尊夫人問好。

1-13

●超好用對話

A：I have something to tell you, Ann.

B：What is it?

A：I lost your book. I'm sorry.

B：Oh, that's OK.

中譯

A：安，我有事情要告訴妳。
B：是什麼事？
A：我把妳的書弄丟了，我很抱歉。
B：喔，沒關係的。

精選單字

have 有	tell 告訴	lost 遺失，弄丟 (lose的過去式)	sorry 對不起，抱歉
something 某事，某物	what 什麼	book 書本	OK 沒關係

1 ■ **I'm <u>sorry</u>.**
我很<u>抱歉</u>。

I'm busy.
■ 我很忙。

I'm poor, but I'm happy.
■ 我很窮，但我很開心。

替換看看

so sorry	very sorry	really sorry
非常抱歉	很抱歉	真的很抱歉
surprised	fine	not sure
很驚訝	很好	不確定

2 ■ **I didn't <u>mean it</u>.**
我不是（沒）<u>故意的</u>。

I didn't order this.
■ 我沒有點這個。

I didn't want to bother you.
■ 那時候我並沒有打擾你的意思。

替換看看

mean to do it	mean to do that	mean to say that
故意那樣做的	故意那樣做的	故意那樣說的
know	order this	hear it
知道	叫這個	聽到

★打開話題的好句子 • • • • • • • • • • • •

■1 我要這樣說 1-15

- **Excuse me.**

  對不起。

- **It's my fault.**

  那是我的錯。

- **Please forgive me.**

  請原諒我。

- **I apologize for troubling you.**

  很抱歉讓你這麼麻煩。

- **Oops! My mistake!**

  唉呦！是我的錯！

■2 你要那樣說

- **Sorry I'm late.**

  抱歉我遲到了。

- **Sorry I didn't call.**

  抱歉我沒打電話過去。

- **Sorry for lying.**

  抱歉我說了謊。

- **That's OK. Don't worry.**

  沒關係，別擔心。

- **I was wrong, too.**

  我也有錯。

UNIT **6** ★ 感謝你這麼親切

 1-16

●超好用對話

A：I can't find my pen. May I use yours?

B：Yes. Here you are.

A：Thank you for your kindness.

B：Not at all.

中譯

A：我找不到我的原子筆。我可以用你的嗎？

B：好啊，拿去。

A：謝謝你這麼好。

B：不客氣。

can't	pen	yours	thank
不可以，不行 (can not的縮寫)	筆	你的	感謝
find	use	here	kindness
找到	使用	這裡	好心

1 ■ **Thank you <u>very much</u>.**
感謝你<u>萬分</u>。

Thank you for seeing me.
■ 謝謝你見我。

Thank you for the gift.
■ 謝謝你的禮物。

替換看看

so much	for your help	for all you've done
萬分	幫助	所做的一切
for everything	for coming	for your kindness
多方關照	能來	你的親切

2 ■ **I had a <u>nice</u> time.**
我度過了一段<u>美好的</u>時光。

You have a bigger car.
■ 你有一台比較大的車子。

You have a small house.
■ 你有一個小房子。

替換看看

lovely	swell	great
可愛的	極好的	很棒的
wonderful	good	happy
美妙的	好的	快樂的

★打開話題的好句子

1 我要這樣說 1-18

■ Thank you for everything.

謝謝你各方面的關照。

■ I enjoyed the movie.

我很喜歡這齣電影。

■ I appreciate your love.

我很感謝你對我的愛。

■ That's just perfect!

那太完美了。

■ I like it very much.

我很喜歡它。

2 你要那樣說

■ You're welcome.

不客氣。

■ My pleasure.

我很榮幸。

■ It was my pleasure.

那是我的榮幸。

■ Not at all.

不客氣。

■ Don't mention it.

快別那麼說了。

●超好用對話

A：I am getting married.

B：Congratulations! What's your wife like?

A：Well, she's a good cook.

B：That's terrific.

A：But she's not good at remembering things.

B：Oh! It'll be all right.

中譯

A：我要結婚了。
B：恭喜！你太太人怎麼樣？
A：這個嘛，她是個烹飪高手。
B：那很棒啊！
A：不過她的記性不太好。
B：是喔？她會變好的啦！

精選單字

get married 結婚	well 嗯	terrific 太棒了	remember 記得
congratulations 恭喜	cook 廚師	good at 擅長於	thing 事情，東西

1 ■ That's <u>great</u>.
那真是<u>太好了</u>。

That's great news.
■ 那真是好消息。

That's pretty cool.
■ 那滿酷的。

替 換 看 看

good	wonderful	nice
好	太棒了	好
interesting	amazing	a good idea
有趣了	了不起	一個好主意

2 ■ Give it <u>a try</u>.
<u>試試看</u>吧。

Give me a minute.
■ 給我一分鐘。

Give me a chance.
■ 給我一個機會。

替 換 看 看

a shot	your best shot	your best
試試看	好好試試看	盡你最大的能力
the old college try	another shot	one last try
盡你最大的能力	再試一次	再試最後一次

★打開話題的好句子

1 我要這樣說

1-21

- That's great!

  那很棒！

- Good job!

  做得好！

- You did it!

  你做到了！

- You look nice.

  你看起來氣色很好！

- I envy you.

  我很嫉妒你。

2 你要那樣說

- I'm sorry to hear that.

  聽到那事我覺得很難過。

- It's not your fault.

  那不是你的錯。

- Cheer up!

  打起精神來！

- Don't worry. I'm here.

  別擔心！我會在你身旁的。

- Everything will be fine.

  一切都會好轉的。

UNIT 8 ★ 那怎麼行，我反對

1-22

●超好用對話

A：That's a wonderful idea.

B：I'm sorry, but I don't think so.

A：I think it's time-saving.

B：Well, that's true.

中譯

A：那點子很棒。
B：抱歉，但我不這麼覺得。
A：我覺得它很省時的。
B：嗯！那倒是真的。

精選單字

wonderful	but	so	saving
美好的	但是	如此	節省
idea	think	time	true
主意，想法	認為，覺得	時間	真的，正確的

1 超好用句型

1 ■ That's <u>true</u>.
那倒是<u>真的</u>。

That's a wonderful idea.
■ 你這個主意挺絕的。

That's a good question.
■ 你這問題問得好。

替 換 看 看

right	interesting	fine with me
對的	有趣的	可以的
a good one	a great idea	possible
好的	很棒的點子	可能

2 ■ You're <u>wrong</u>.
你<u>錯了</u>。

You're hopeless!
■ 你沒救了！

You're crazy.
■ 你瘋了。

替 換 看 看

off	dead wrong	way off base
錯了	錯得離譜了	大錯特錯了
missing the boat	absolutely wrong	lying through your teeth
錯失良機	完全錯了	謊話連篇

★打開話題的好句子 • • • • • • •

■**1** 我要這樣說 ◯ 1-24

- ■I agree.

  我同意。

- ■Yes, I think so too.

  對的，我也這麼認為。

- ■I think you're right.

  我認為你是對的。

- ■Sounds good.

  聽起來很不賴啊！

- ■I'm in.

  我加入。

■**2** 你要那樣說

- ■I don't agree.

  我不同意。

- ■That's impossible.

  那不可能的。

- ■I don't think so.

  我不這麼認為。

- ■You're wrong.

  你錯了。

- ■Please think it over.

  請重新考慮一下。

●超好用對話

A：Happy birthday, Mary! This is for you.

B：Oh, thank you. Can I open it?

A：Sure. Go ahead.

B：Oh, This is just what I've wanted. Thank you so much.

A：You're welcome. I'm glad you like it.

中譯

A：生日快樂！瑪莉！這送給妳。
B：喔！謝謝你！我可以打開嗎？
A：可以啊，打開看看。
B：哇！這正是我一直想要的，太謝謝你了。
A：不客氣。我很高興妳喜歡。

精選單字

happy	open	just	so much
快樂的	打開	剛好，正巧	很，非常地
birthday	go ahead	want	welcome
生日	開始，進行	想要	歡迎

1 超好用句型

1 ■ **Happy <u>birthday</u>!**
生日快樂！

Happy New Year!
■ 新年快樂！

Merry Christmas!
■ 聖誕節快樂！

替換看看

Anniversary	Halloween	Valentine's Day
週年紀念	萬聖節前夕	情人節
Father's Day	Mother's Day	Thanksgiving
父親節	母親節	感恩節

2 ■ **I wish you <u>happiness</u>!**
我祝你快樂！

I wish you all the best.
■ 我祝你一切都好。

I wish you luck.
■ 我祝你好運。

替換看看

success	good luck	good health
成功	幸運	健康
the best of everything	good luck in your work	a Merry Xmas and a Happy New Year
一切順利	工作幸運	聖誕快樂跟新年快樂

★打開話題的好句子

1 我要這樣說 1-27

- Congratulations!

  恭喜！

- Happy birthday!

  生日快樂！

- You must be happy.

  你一定很快樂！

- You finally did it.

  你終於做到了！

- Wow! That's wonderful!

  哇！那真是太棒了！

2 你要那樣說

- I see.

  我瞭解。

- Really?

  真的嗎？

- Unbelievable!

  真不敢相信！

- I guess so.

  我猜是這樣吧。

- No wonder.

  難怪。

UNIT 10 ★ 麻煩再說一次

1-28

● 超好用對話

A：Look at that bird, Dad.

B：Wow! What a small bird! How cute!

A：Can I keep it?

B：No, Mary, you can't.

中譯

A：你看那隻鳥，爸爸。
B：哇！好小的鳥喔！真可愛！
A：我可以把牠帶回去嗎？
B：不，瑪莉，妳不行。

精選單字

look 看	bird 小鳥	wow 哇	cute 可愛的
that 那個	dad 父親	small 小的	keep 保留

1 超好用句型

1 ■ Could you please <u>speak slower</u>?
可以請你<u>說慢一點</u>嗎？

Could you please keep quiet?
■ 可以請你保持安靜嗎？

Could you please bring me a glass of water?
■ 可以請你拿一杯水給我嗎？

替換看看

speak louder	write it down	spell that
說大聲一點	把它寫下來	拼出那個字
tell me the time	stop doing that	leave me alone
告訴我時間	別再那麼做了	別管我

2 ■ I'd like to <u>send a postcard</u>.
我想要<u>寄一張明信片</u>。

I'd like to see a timetable.
■ 我想要看時刻表。

I'd like to rent a car.
■ 我想要租一輛車。

替換看看

see a doctor	try skiing	buy a swimsuit
看醫生	嘗試滑雪	買游泳衣
pay by credit card	return this	get off here
刷卡付費	歸還這個	在這裡下車

★打開話題的好句子

1 我要這樣說

 1-30

■ **Please.**

拜託你。

■ **Please help me.**

請幫助我。

■ **May I ask your phone number?**

我可以跟你要電話嗎？

■ **Would you do it for me?**

你可以幫我做嗎？

■ **I'm begging you.**

我求你。

2 你要那樣說

■ **Can I keep it?**

我可以留著它嗎？

■ **I don't understand.**

我不懂。

■ **No smoking, please.**

請不要抽煙。

■ **May I try this on?**

我可以試穿這件嗎？

■ **Shall I open the windows?**

要我打開窗戶嗎？

●超好用對話

A：Excuse me. I'm lost. Can you help me?

B：Sure. Where do you want to go?

A：Taipei Station.

B：OK. Keep walking and turn left at the next corner. It's on the right.

A：Thank you.

B：You're welcome.

中譯

A：不好意思，我迷路了，你可以幫幫我嗎？
B：當然可以。你想要去哪裡？
A：台北車站。
B：好，繼續走，在下一個路口左轉。它就在右手邊。
A：謝謝你。
B：不客氣。

精選單字

lost	station	walk	left
迷路的	車站	走路	左邊

Taipei	keep	turn	corner
台北	保持，持續	轉彎	角落，轉角

1 超好用句型

1 ■ **Where is <u>the post office</u>?**
郵局在哪裡？

Where is my car?
■ 我的車在哪裡？

Where are your children?
■ 你的孩子們在哪裡？

替換看看

Central Park	the nearest subway station	Hyatt Hotel
中央公園	最近的地鐵站	君悅飯店
parking lot	the outlet market	the art museum
停車場	特賣會場	美術館

2 ■ **How do I get to <u>the airport</u>?**
我要如何到機場去呢？

How do I start the car?
■ 我要如何啟動車子？

How do you spell that?
■ 那個字要怎麼拚啊？

替換看看

the train station	City Hall	Meiji Palace
火車站	市政府	明治神宮
Sienna	the Grand Canyon	the beach
西亞那	大峽谷	海灘

★打開話題的好句子

■1 我要這樣說

 1-33

■ Excuse me!

不好意思！

■ Where's the train station?

火車站在哪裡？

■ Where are you going?

你要去哪裡？

■ Please show me where we are.

請告訴我我們現在的所在位置。

■ Is it far to the airport?

那兒離機場很遠嗎？

■2 你要那樣說

■ Go straight.

直走。

■ Turn left at the second corner.

第二個路口左轉。

■ It's on your left.

它就在你的左手邊。

■ You can't miss it.

你不可能找不到的。

■ Keep walking for three blocks.

繼續走，走過三個路口。

UNIT 2 ★ 怎麼坐車還有租車呢 🎧 1-34

● 超好用對話

A：What time will the bus leave?

B：It leaves at four.

A：Then we have half an hour to wait.

Shall we buy something to drink?

B：Good idea.

中譯

A：巴士什麼時候會開？
B：四點會開。
A：那我們還有半小時要等。我們去買個東西喝好嗎？
B：好主意。

精選單字

bus	four	hour	buy
巴士，公車	四 (at four =四點鐘)	小時	購買
leave	half	wait	drink
離開	一半	等候	喝

1-35

1 超好用句型

1 ■ **Let's go by <u>bus</u>.**
我們搭<u>公車</u>去吧。

Let's finish the page.
■ 我們把這頁看完吧。

Let's try again.
■ 我們再試一次看看。

替換看看

car	MRT	train
汽車	捷運	電車
subway	bus	taxi
地鐵	公車	計程車

2 ■ **Do you have any <u>compact</u> cars?**
請問你們有<u>小型車</u>嗎？

Do you have the number?
■ 你有電話號碼嗎？

Do you have a job?
■ 你有工作嗎？

替換看看

economy	mid-sized	full-sized
省油的	中型的	最大型的
Japanese	4-door	automatic
日本的	四門的	自排的

★打開話題的好句子 · · · · · · · · · · · · · · · ·

∎1 我要這樣說 1-36

- Where are you going?

  你要去哪裡？

- How can I get to Taipei Station?

  我要如何才能到達台北車站呢？

- Which line should I take to go to down town?

  我要搭哪一線才能到市中心呢？

- Take the blue line. It's an express train.

  搭藍線，那是特快車。

- That's the nearest stop.

  那是最接近的停靠站了。

∎2 你要那樣說

- Where can I buy a ticket?

  我在哪裡可以買到票呢？

- I'm going to Central Park.

  我準備要去中央公園。

- How much is it to Central Park?

  到中央公園要多少錢？

- It's sixty dollars.

  要六十元。

- A ticket to West 8th Street, Please.

  一張到第八西街的票，謝謝。

●超好用對話

A：Excuse me, which train goes to London?

B：That orange one over there.

A：I see. Thank you.

B：You're welcome.

中譯

A：不好意思，請問哪一班車是到倫敦的？
B：那邊那一輛橘色的。
A：我知道了，謝謝你。
B：不客氣。

精選單字

excuse me	train	London	there
不好意思	火車	倫敦	那邊
which	go	orange	see
哪一個	去	橘色的	看見；明白

1 超好用句型

1 ■ Which <u>line</u> should we <u>take</u>?
我們該坐哪一線？

Which one will you choose?
■ 你會選擇哪一樣？

Which way do you want to go?
■ 你想要走哪個方向？

替 換 看 看

platform／go to 月台／去	path／take 路／走	car／get on 車廂／上車
stop／get off 站／下車	way／go 方向／去	seat／take 座位／坐

2 ■ What's the <u>departure time</u>?
出發時間是？

What is the reason?
■ 為了什麼原因？

What is the matter?
■ 怎麼了？

替 換 看 看

arrival time 抵達時間	best route 最佳路線	difference 差別
speed limit 速限	next stop 下一站	terminal station 終點站

★打開話題的好句子

1 我要這樣說

 1-39

- Where's the train for London?

  往倫敦的火車在哪裡？

- Go down(up) the stairs.

  往樓下（上）走。

- Take the train with green stripes.

  搭乘有綠色條紋的那班火車。

- It's on the 4th platform.

  在第四月台。

- You need to change trains here.

  你得在這裡換車。

2 你要那樣說

- What's the next station?

  下一站是？

- It's the terminal station.

  是終點站。

- Where do you get off?

  你在哪裡下車啊？

- Don't sit on the priority seats.

  不要坐在博愛座上。

- Excuse me. This is my seat.

  不好意思，這是我的座位。

UNIT 4 ★ 我必須搭紅線嗎

1-40

● 超好用對話

A：Excuse me. Which subway should I take to Green Road?

B：Go to platform 2 and take the red line.

A：How many stops are there from here to Green Road?

B：5 stops.

中譯

A：不好意思，我應該要搭哪一班車才能到格林路呢？
B：到第二月台，然後搭紅線。
A：從這裡到格林路有幾站呢？
B：五站。

subway 地鐵	green 綠色的	platform 月台	line 線
take 搭乘	road 馬路	red 紅色的	stop 車站；站牌

47

1 超好用句型

1 ■ **Where is the <u>subway station</u>?**
地鐵站在哪裡？

Where are our bags?
■ 我們的包包在哪裡？

Where is it located?
■ 它位在哪裡？

替 換 看 看

entrance	exit	ticket machine
入口	出口	購票機
fare adjustment office	information desk	box office
票價調整處	詢問處	購票處

2 ■ **You have to change to <u>the red</u> line.**
你必須轉搭紅線。

We have to cook dinner.
■ 我們得做晚飯了。

I have to work.
■ 我得工作。

替 換 看 看

Danshui	Xindian	Zhonghe
淡水	新店	中和
Muzha	Ginza	Marunouchi
木柵	銀座	丸之內

★打開話題的好句子 · · · · · ·

1-42

1 我要這樣說

■ Where's the nearest subway station?

最近的地鐵站在哪裡？

■ Does this subway go to Central Park?

這班地鐵有到中央公園嗎？

■ Where do I transfer?

我要在哪裡轉車？

■ The exit is on the right.

出口在右邊。

■ Take the next train .

搭下一班車。

2 你要那樣說

■ How many stops to Gig Garden?

還要過幾站才會到吉格花園？

■ Can I have a subway map?

可以給我一張地鐵圖嗎？

■ How late does the subway run?

地鐵行駛到多晚呢？

■ Is this a local train?

這是普通車嗎？

■ Which exit should I take to the SEA hotel?

我要走哪一個出口才會到SEA飯店呢？

● 超好用對話

A：Excuse me, sir. What's the next stop?

B：It's the National Taiwan University.

A：Then…does this bus stop at Taipei Main Station?

B：I don't think so. I think you took the wrong bus.

A：Oh, no!

中譯

A：先生，不好意思，請問下一站是？
B：是國立台灣大學。
A：那...這輛車有停台北火車站嗎？
B：恐怕沒有，我想你搭錯公車了。
A：喔，不！

精選單字

next	Taiwan	main	think
下一個	台灣	主要的	想，認為

national	university	station	wrong
國家的	大學	車站	錯誤的

1 超好用句型

1 ■ Where can I catch a/an <u>No.33</u> bus?
我在哪裡可以搭到33號公車呢？

Where can I get my baggage?
■ 我可以在哪裡拿我的行李呢？

Where can I buy some shoes?
■ 我可以在哪裡買鞋呢？

替換看看

double-decker	sight-seeing	airport
雙層的	觀光	機場
No.226	shuttle	community
226號	接駁車	社區公車

2 ■ Does this bus stop at <u>Hight Street</u>?
這班公車有停海特街嗎？

Does this train go to Daly City?
■ 這班火車有到達利市嗎？

Does this price include tax?
■ 這個價錢有含稅嗎？

替換看看

Balboa Park	National Taiwan University	the zoo
巴爾波亞公園	國立台灣大學	動物園
downtown	Geary Street	NTU hospital
市中心	基利街	臺大醫院

★打開話題的好句子　· · · · · · · · · · · ·

  1-45

■ Where can I get on a bus to the airport?

我可以在哪裡搭公車到機場去呢？

■ Is this to the Zhongxiaofuxing intersection?

這是往忠孝復興路口的嗎？

■ I'll ask the driver for you.

我幫你問一下司機。

■ There are four more stops.

還有四站。

■ Don't forget your stuff.

別忘了你的東西。

2 你要那樣說

■ Don't sit in the priority seats, please.

請不要坐在博愛座上。

■ What's the next stop?

下一站是什麼？

■ Am I on the right bus?

我搭對車了嗎？

■ I think you took the wrong bus.

我想你搭錯車了。

■ Get off at next stop and take No.311.

在下一站下車，然後改搭311號。

UNIT 6 ★ 司機先生，我到中央公園

1-46

●超好用對話

A：Where to, sir?

B：To the airport, please.

A：OK, sir.

B：Drive faster, please. We must
get there before 10:00.

A：No problem, sir.

中譯

A：到哪裡呢，先生？
B：麻煩到機場。
A：好的，先生。
B：麻煩你開快一點，我們在十
點以前一定要到達那裡。
A：沒問題，先生。

精選單字

where 哪裡	airport 機場	faster 快一點	get 抵達
to 到	drive 開車，駕駛	must 必須	before 之前

1 超好用句型

1 ■ **Please take me to <u>the airport</u>.**
請帶我去機場。

Please take me to the emergency room.
■ 請帶我去急診室。

Please take me to this place.
■ 請到我去這個地方。

替換看看

the hospital	the theater	the police station
醫院	劇院	警察局
the Grand Hotel	the harbor	the church
圓山飯店	港口	教堂

2 ■ **We must <u>go</u> now.**
我們現在得走了。

We must be there soon.
■ 我們得火速到達那裡。

We must ask him.
■ 我們得問問他。

替換看看

talk	leave	hurry
談談	離開	快點
stop	turn	pull over
停下來	轉彎	靠邊停

1 我要這樣說

 1-48

■ Where can I get a taxi?

我在哪裡可以搭到計程車？

■ Where's the taxi stand?

計程車站在哪裡？

■ Please take me to this address.

請帶我到這個地址去。

■ Available taxis have a red light.

可搭乘的計程車會有個紅色的燈。

■ To Macy's, please.

麻煩到梅西百貨公司。

2 你要那樣說

■ How much?

多少錢？

■ Keep the change.

不用找了。

■ Drive faster, please.

請開快一點。

■ I'm in a hurry.

我在趕時間。

■ Can we get there in ten minutes?

我們可以在十分鐘內到那裡嗎？

●超好用對話

A：Hello.

B：Hello. This is Mary speaking. May I talk to George, please?

A：I'm sorry. He's out now.

B：Would you tell him that I called?

A：Sure, I will.

B：Thank you. Good-bye.

中譯

A：喂。
B：喂，我是瑪麗，我可以和喬治說話嗎？
A：不好意思，他現在不在家喔。
B：你可以轉告他說我有打電話來嗎？
A：當然，我會的。
B：謝謝你，再見。

精選單字

speak	please	now	call
說話	請	現在	打電話給…
talk	out	tell	good-bye
談話	出去；外出	告訴	再見

1 ■ **May I speak to Smith?**
我可以和史密斯說話嗎？

May I close the window?
■ 我可以把窗戶關上嗎？

May I come in?
■ 我可以進來嗎？

替換看看

speak to a sales person	talk to your manager	talk to your section chief
和業務員說話	和你的經理說話	和你們部門的負責人說話
ask where he went	leave a message	have your name
問他去了哪裡	留個口信	請教您的大名

2 ■ **Please tell him to call me at home.**
請叫（告訴）他打我家裡的電話。

Please tell him to call Bill.
■ 請叫他打給比爾。

Please tell her I said hello.
■ 請幫我向她問好。

替換看看

to call my cell phone	that I called	that I will call again
打我的手機	我有打來	我會再打過來
that I will be late	to call me back	that Jessica wants to speak to him
我會遲到	回我電話	潔西卡想跟他談談

★打開話題的好句子

1 我要這樣說　　1-51

- **Hello!**

  喂！

- **May I speak to Sandra, please?**

  我可以和珊卓拉說話嗎？

- **This is Helen speaking.**

  我是海倫。

- **Can you talk now?**

  你現在方便說話嗎？

- **Sorry to call you at dinner time.**

  很抱歉在晚餐的時間打電話給你。

2 你要那樣說

- **When will he be back?**

  他什麼時候會回來？

- **May I leave a message?**

  我可以留個口信嗎？

- **I see. I'll call again.**

  我知道了。我會再打電話過來的。

- **Please tell him that I called.**

  請轉告他說我有打來。

- **My phone number is 02-1234-5678.**

  我的電話是02-1234-5678。

UNIT 2 ★ 她正在洗澡，你晚點再打

 1-52

A：Lisa Parker's office.

B：Hi, this is James, Lisa's husband. Can I speak to her, please?

A：I'm sorry, Mr. Parker. Lisa is out now. Would you like to leave a message?

B：Well…when is she coming back?

A：She should be back in two hours.

中譯

A：莉莎派克辦公室。
B：嗨，我是莉莎的先生詹姆斯。我可以跟她說個話嗎？
A：很抱歉，派克先生，莉莎現在不在。您要留言給她嗎？
B：嗯…她什麼時候會回來？
A：她應該在兩小時之內會回來。

精選單字

office 辦公室	leave 留下	when 何時	two 二
husband 丈夫	message 訊息	come back 回來	hour 小時

1 ■ She's <u>out right now</u>.
她<u>現在不在</u>。

She's in the middle of a meeting.
■ 她正在開會。

She's not home at this moment.
■ 她現在不在家。

替 換 看 看

not here	in the bath now	out with her friends
不在這裡	正在洗澡	和她的朋友出去了
on another line	away from her desk	not available
正在通電話	不在位子上	無法接聽電話

2 ■ She should be back <u>soon</u>.
她應該<u>很快</u>就會回來了。

I should be back by then.
■ 我那時候應該就回來了。

They should be here by noon.
■ 他們應該中午就到這裡了。

替 換 看 看

in a little while	in a couple of hours	by three
再過一會兒	再過幾個小時	三點以前
by dinner	real soon	before ten o'clock
晚餐以前	很快	十點以前

★打開話題的好句子

1 我要這樣說

1-54

■ Who is calling?

你是哪位？

■ Would you speak more slowly?

你可以說慢一點嗎？

■ She went to work today.

她今天去上班了。

■ I don't know what time she'll be back.

我不曉得她幾點會回來。

■ Shall I have him call you back?

我請他回電給你好嗎？

2 你要那樣說

■ May I take a message?

我替你留個口信好嗎？

■ I'll tell him that you called.

我會轉告他說你有打電話過來的。

■ Does he know your number?

他知道你的電話號碼嗎？

■ One moment, please.

請稍等一下。

■ Please hold.

請稍等一下。

●超好用對話

A：Hello?

B：Hello. This is Mary. Can I speak to George?

A：I'm afraid you have the wrong number.

B：Is this 25-8844?

A：No, it isn't.

B：Oh, I'm sorry. Thank you.

中譯

A：喂？
B：喂，我是瑪麗，可以請喬治聽電話嗎？
A：我想你打錯電話了。
B：這裡是25-8844嗎？
A：不，並不是。
B：噢，我很抱歉。謝謝你。

精選單字

hello 哈囉	afraid 害怕	wrong 錯誤的	sorry 對不起，抱歉
speak 說話	have 有	number 數字，號碼	thank 感謝

1 超好用句型

1 ■ <u>I am sorry</u> , I called the wrong number.
我<u>很抱歉</u>，我撥錯電話了。

I'm sorry, who's calling?
■ 不好意思，你是哪位？

I'm sorry to hear the news.
■ 聽到這消息，我深感遺憾。

替換看看

Sorry	I apologize	I guess
抱歉	我道歉	我猜想
Excuse me	I think I made a mistake	I'm terribly sorry
不好意思	我想我弄錯了	我真的非常抱歉

2 ■ Is this <u>25-8844</u>?
這裡是<u>25-8844</u>嗎？

Is this for sale?
■ 這些是在拍賣的嗎？

Is this for women?
■ 這是給女性的嗎？

替換看看

Miss Glen's house	Mrs. Kent's office	an English school
格蘭小姐家	肯特太太的辦公室	一間英語學校
the sales department	Carter's Grocery Store	the principal's office
銷售部	卡特雜貨店	校長辦公室

★打開話題的好句子 • • • • • • • • • • • • •

■1 我要這樣說

- **Sorry, you have the wrong number.**

  抱歉，你打錯電話了。

- **What number did you call?**

  你撥幾號呢？

- **There's no Terry here.**

  這裡沒有泰瑞這個人。

- **You should check the number again.**

  你應該再檢查一次電話號碼。

- **Who are you calling?**

  你要找誰？

■2 你要那樣說

- **Sorry, I called the wrong number.**

  抱歉，我打錯電話了。

- **Is this 02-1234-4678?**

  這裡是02-1234-4678嗎？

- **Is this an English school?**

  這裡是間英語學校嗎？

- **I'm sorry.**

  我很抱歉。

- **That's okay.**

  沒關係。

UNIT 4 ★ 明天晚上如何

 1-58

●超好用對話

A：Do you have time next Friday?

B：I'm free then. What's up?

A：We are having a party. Do you want to come?

B：I'd love to. Should I bring anything?

A：Nope. We'll take care of it.

＼ 中譯

> A：下個禮拜五，你有空嗎？
> B：我那時候有空。什麼事？
> A：我們要辦一個派對，你要來嗎？
> B：我很樂意。我應該帶些什麼東西嗎？
> A：不用，我們會打理好一切的。

time 時間	Friday 星期五	what's up 什麼事	bring 帶
next 下一個	free 自由的，空閒的	party 派對	anything 任何事物

1 ■ Do you have time next <u>Friday</u>?
下個禮拜五你有空嗎？

Do you have a vacant room?
■ 你有空房間嗎？

Do you have road maps?
■ 你有道路地圖嗎？

替換看看

Sunday	Monday	Tuesday	Wednesday
星期天	星期一	星期二	星期三
Thursday	Friday	Saturday	
星期四	星期五	星期六	

2 ■ I'll be there by <u>seven o'clock</u>.
我七點之前會到那裡。

I'll be there before 9:00 p.m.
■ 我晚上九點之前會到那裡。

I'll be here for another hour.
■ 我還會在這裡待一個小時。

替換看看

three o'clock	four o'clock	six o'clock
三點鐘	四點鐘	六點鐘
seven o'clock	eight o'clock	eleven o'clock
七點鐘	八點鐘	十一點鐘

★打開話題的好句子

▌1 我要這樣說

 1-60

- **Are you free next Monday?**

  下禮拜一你有空嗎？

- **Let's go out for dinner.**

  我們出去吃個晚餐吧。

- **My parents want to meet you.**

  我的父母想要見見你。

- **Sure. I'd love to.**

  當然，我很願意。

- **Sorry. I'll be busy next week.**

  抱歉，我下禮拜很忙。

▌2 你要那樣說

- **When shall we meet?**

  我們什麼時候見面呢？

- **How about tomorrow night?**

  明天晚上如何？

- **It's up to you.**

  看你囉。（你決定囉）

- **I'll check my schedule.**

  我會看一下我的行程。

- **Let's meet at the station.**

  我們在車站碰面吧。

1-61

●超好用對話

A：Come on in, Susan! Your room is over there.

B：Thanks, John. I had a hard time finding your house, actually.

A：Why didn't you call me, then?

B：I didn't have my cell phone with me.

A：I see. Well, just tell me if you need anything.

中譯

A：請進，蘇珊，妳的房間在那邊。
B：謝謝，約翰。其實我花了好大的功夫才找到你家呢。
A：那妳為什麼沒打電話給我呢？
B：我沒有帶我的手機。
A：我懂了。那麼，如果妳需要什麼就跟我說吧。

精選單字

room	hard	house	If
房間	很難的	房子	如果，假使
over there	find	cell phone	need
在那邊	找到	手機	需要

1 超好用句型

1 ■ **Why don't you <u>get a cab</u>?**
你為什麼不<u>叫輛計程車</u>呢?

Why don't you come with us?
■ 你為什麼不和我們一起去呢?

Why don't you try on this shirt?
■ 你何不試穿看看這件襯衫呢?

替 換 看 看

come in	call me to pick you up	stay for dinner
進來	打電話叫我去接你	留下來吃晚餐
join us	call her	go home
加入我們	打電話給她	回家

2 ■ **If you <u>get lost</u>, please call me.**
如果你<u>迷路</u>了,請打電話給我。

If you didn't do that, please tell me.
■ 如果那不是你做的,請你告訴我。

If you don't take that job, please let me know.
■ 如果你不要接受那份工作,請跟我說一聲。

替 換 看 看

need anything	can come	have time
需要任何東西	可以來	有時間
are in trouble	want to talk	forgive me
有麻煩	想要聊天	原諒我

★打開話題的好句子

1 我要這樣說

1-63

- Take the Worcester Line and get off at the first stop.

  搭渥斯特線，然後在第一個停靠站下車。

- Let's meet at the front door.

  我們在前門碰面吧。

- Please call me when you arrive.

  你到的時候請打電話給我。

- I'll draw you a map.

  我畫張地圖給你。

- If you get lost, please call me.

  如果你迷路的話，請打電話給我。

2 你要那樣說

- Please come on in.

  請進。

- Take off your shoes here, please.

  麻煩請在這裡脫鞋子。

- Please have a seat.

  請坐。

- Please make yourself at home.

  請把這裡當自己的家。（隨意）

- This is from my husband.

  這是我丈夫給的（禮物）。

UNIT 6 ★ 你家好棒喔

1-64

●超好用對話

A：Welcome, Mary. Come on in.

B：Thank you for your invitation.

A：The pleasure is ours. Have a seat, please.

B：Thank you.

A：This is our living room.

B：Wow! Nice house! The table looks beautiful.

中譯

A：歡迎啊，瑪麗。請進。
B：謝謝你的邀請。
A：那是我們的榮幸。請坐。
B：謝謝你。
A：這裡是我們的客廳。
B：哇！好棒的房子！桌子好漂亮。

精選單字

invitation 邀請	ours 我們的	living room 客廳	table 桌子
pleasure 榮幸	seat 坐位(have a seat 請坐)	nice 很好的	beautiful 漂亮的

1 超好用句型

1 ■ Nice <u>house</u>!
好棒的<u>房子</u>！

Nice day!
■ 好棒的一天！

Nice shirt!
■ 好棒的襯衫！

替換看看

car	curtains	living room
車	窗簾	客廳
garden	bedroom	dress
院子	臥房	洋裝

2 ■ You have a/an <u>beautiful home</u>.
你有一間很<u>漂亮的家</u>。

We have two tickets.
■ 我們有兩張票。

She has a camera.
■ 她有一台相機。

替換看看

lovely daughter	big house	cute dog
很可愛的女兒	很大的房子	很可愛的狗
wonderful garden	amazing cook	really nice sofa
很棒的院子	很厲害的廚師	很棒的沙發

★打開話題的好句子 · · · · · · · · · · · ·

1 我要這樣說

1-66

■ **Good evening!**
晚安！

■ **Thank you for inviting me.**
謝謝你邀請我。

■ **I'm sorry that I'm a little late(early).**
抱歉我來晚（早）了一點。

■ **You live in a nice place.**
你家真是不錯。

■ **Should I put my shoes outside?**
我是不是應該把鞋子放在外面呢？

■ **This is a small present.**
這是個小禮物。

2 你要那樣說

■ **Hello! Please come in.**
哈囉！請進。

■ **Please hang your overcoat here.**
請把你的大衣掛在這裡。

■ **I'm glad you like it.**
我很高興你喜歡。

■ **The other guests are in the library.**
其他的客人都在圖書館裡。

■ **Make yourself at home.**
把這裡當自己家吧。

UNIT 7 ★ 我有一個兒子和一隻狗 1-67

●超好用對話

A：This is a picture of my family.

B：Who is this little boy?

A：He is my nephew. He is three years old.

B：He is lovely. What is his name?

A：His name is Tom.

中譯

A：這是一張我家人的照片。
B：這個小男孩是誰？
A：他是我的姪子，他三歲大。
B：他真是可愛，他叫什麼名字啊？
A：他的名字叫湯姆。

精選
單字

picture 照片，圖片	little 小的	nephew 姪子	year(s) old 歲
family 家人	boy 男孩	three 三	lovely 可愛的

1 超好用句型

1 ■ I have <u>two daughters</u>.

我有<u>兩個女兒</u>。

I have two dogs.

■ 我有（養）兩隻狗。

I have no money.

■ 我沒有錢。

替換看看

a beautiful wife	three kids	a pet cat
一個美麗的妻子	三個小孩	一隻寵物貓
two cousins	a lot of friends	only one son
兩個表/堂兄弟姊妹	很多朋友	一個獨生子

2 ■ <u>Jeff</u>, this is <u>Ana</u>. <u>Ana</u>, this is <u>Jeff</u>.

<u>傑夫</u>，這位是<u>安娜</u>。<u>安娜</u>，這位是<u>傑夫</u>。

This is Jenny.

■ 這位是珍妮。

Ken, this is Mr. Brown. Mr. Brown, this is Ken.

■ 肯，這位是布朗先生。布朗先生，這位是肯。

替換看看

Kate／Susan ／Susan／Kate	Ben／my dad ／Dad／Ben	Joe／Mr. Carson ／Mr. Carson／Joe
凱特／蘇珊／蘇珊／凱特	班／我爸爸／爸爸／班	喬／卡森先生／卡森先生／喬
Lisa／my mom／Mom ／my friend, Lisa	George／Emma ／Emma／George	Frank／Mrs. Hsieh ／Mrs. Hsieh／Frank
麗莎／我媽媽／媽媽／我的朋友麗莎	喬治／艾瑪／艾瑪／喬治	法蘭克／謝太太／謝太太／法蘭克

★打開話題的好句子

■1 我要這樣說　　1-69

- **Let me introduce my family.**

  讓我來介紹一下我的家人。

- **This is Edward. He is my brother.**

  這位是艾德華。他是我弟弟（哥哥）。

- **I have two sons and a daughter.**

  我有兩個兒子、一個女兒。

- **My father isn't home today.**

  我爸爸今天不在家。

- **My husband works for Google.**

  我丈夫在Google工作。

■2 你要那樣說

- **Both my parents work.**

  我的父母都在工作。

- **Our son is studying abroad.**

  我們的兒子在海外唸書。

- **My brother is three years older than me.**

  我哥哥比我大三歲。

- **We look alike.**

  我們長得很像。

- **We are the opposite.**

  我們完全南轅北轍。

UNIT 8 ★ 嚐嚐看！這是我拿手的菜

1-70

●超好用對話

A：Dinner is ready!

B：What are we having for dinner?

A：Steak!

B：Wow! It looks delicious.

A：I hope you will like it.

B：Don't worry. Steak is my favorite.

■■■中譯

A：晚餐好囉！
B：我們今天晚餐吃什麼呢？
A：吃牛排。
B：哇！看起來真好吃。
A：我希望你會喜歡這料理。
B：別擔心，牛排是我的最愛。

精選單字

dinner	steak	delicious	worry
晚餐	牛排	美味的	擔心

ready	look	hope	favorite
準備好的	看，看起來	希望	最喜愛的

1 ■ It is <u>delicious</u>.
這真（太）<u>好吃了</u>。

It is wonderful.
■ 這太神奇了。

It is almost ready.
■ 差不多可以用餐了。

替 換 看 看

too sweet	crispy	expensive
甜了	酥脆	貴了
hot	good	broken
燙	棒了	壞掉了

2 ■ Would you please pass me the <u>pepper</u>?
可以麻煩你拿<u>胡椒粉</u>給我嗎？

Would you please sit down?
■ 請你坐下。

Would you please pass the rolls around?
■ 可以請你把小麵包傳給大家嗎？

替 換 看 看

salt	butter	bread
鹽巴	奶油	麵包
salad	milk	dish
沙拉	牛奶	盤子

★打開話題的好句子

1 我要這樣說

 1-72

■ It's time to eat.

該吃飯了。

■ It smells good!

好香喔!

■ Would you please pass me the salt?

請幫我拿一下鹽巴。

■ Here you are!

給你。

■ Would you like some more?

你還要再來一些嗎?

2 你要那樣說

■ I hope you'd like Taiwanese food.

我希望你會喜歡台灣料理。

■ That's my favorite.

那是我最愛吃的。

■ You cook very well.

你真會煮菜。

■ Would you give me the recipe?

可以給我食譜嗎?

■ I'm so full.

我吃得好飽。

●超好用對話

A：There are many people here.

B：Nice party, isn't it?

A：Yes, it is. By the way, do you know that girl?

B：Yes. She's my friend, Mary.

A：Will you introduce me to her?

B：Sure, no problem.

中譯

A：這裡人真多。
B：很棒的派對，不是嗎？
A：是啊。對了，你認識那個女生嗎？
B：認識啊，她是我朋友瑪麗。
A：可以把我介紹給她認識嗎？
B：當然，沒問題。

精選單字

many	party	girl	introduce
很多的	派對	女生	介紹
people	by the way	friend	problem
人	順帶一提，對了	朋友	問題

1 超好用句型

1 ■ **May I <u>join you</u>?**
我可以<u>加入你們</u>嗎？

May I have another beer?
■ 我可以再要一瓶啤酒嗎？

May I put my seat back?
■ 我可以把椅子往後靠嗎？

替換看看

get in	see that	try it
進來	看看那個	試試看
sit here	buy you a drink	talk to you
坐這裡	請你喝杯飲料	跟你說話

2 ■ **<u>Nice party</u>, isn't it?**
很棒的一場派對，對吧？

It's interesting, isn't it?
■ 那真是有趣，對吧？

That's a good idea, isn't it?
■ 那真是個好主意，對吧？

替換看看

Great party	Nice song	Excellent food
很棒的派對	很棒的歌	很棒的食物
A wonderful night	Good idea	Great show
一個美好的夜晚	好主意	很棒的表演

★打開話題的好句子　· · · · · · · · · · · · ·

▊1 我要這樣說　🔘1-75

■ **Please introduce me to your friends.**

請把我介紹給你的朋友們。

■ **I'm so pleased to meet you.**

我非常高興認識你。

■ **Please call me Ken.**

請叫我肯。

■ **I'm Debra. You can just call me Deb.**

我是黛博拉。你可以叫我小黛。

■ **I've heard a lot about you.**

我聽說了很多你的事蹟。

▊2 你要那樣說

■ **May I join you?**

我可以加入你們嗎？

■ **Is this seat taken?**

這裡有人坐嗎？

■ **Can I buy you a drink?**

我可以請你喝杯飲料嗎？

■ **Do you have a light?**

你有打火機嗎？

■ **Let's play pool.**

我們來打撞球吧。

UNIT 10 ★ 我喜歡假日 騎單車到郊外

1-76

●超好用對話

A：What do you do, Tom?

B：I study in law school.

A：So, are you going to be a lawyer?

B：Yes, of course.

A：That's wonderful.

B：What about you? What do you do?

A：I'm a writer.

■■中譯

A：你是做什麼的，湯姆？
B：我在法學院唸書。
A：那麼你以後要當個律師囉？
B：是啊，當然。
A：那很棒啊。
B：那麼你呢？你是做什麼的？
A：我是個作家。

精選單字

study 學習，研讀	school 學校	of course 當然	about 關於
law 法律	lawyer 律師	wonderful 美好的	writer 作家

1 ■ I like <u>your hair</u>.
我喜歡<u>你的頭髮</u>。

I like skiing and tennis.
■ 我喜歡滑雪和網球。

I like it very much.
■ 我好喜歡這個。

替換看看

your dress	sports	classical music
你的洋裝	運動	古典樂
talking to you	your magic tricks	this coat
和你聊天	你的魔術	這件外套

2 ■ How's <u>your family</u>?
<u>你的家人</u>還好嗎？

How's Mary?
■ 瑪麗還好嗎？

How's everything?
■ 一切都還好嗎？

替換看看

your mother	your job	your steak
你母親	你的工作	你的牛排
the food	work	your weekend
食物	工作	你的週末

★打開話題的好句子

1 我要這樣說

1-78

- What do you do?

  你是做什麼的？

- I'd like to hear about it.

  我想聽聽相關的事情。

- I'm interested.

  我很有興趣。

- How did it go?

  進行得如何？

- That's great.

  那太好了。

2 你要那樣說

- Would you like to dance?

  你想要跳舞嗎？

- That's a pretty dress.

  那洋裝真漂亮。

- What's your sign?

  你是什麼星座的？

- Don't I know you from somewhere?

  我是不是在哪個地方見過你啊？

- Do you mind if I smoke?

  你介意我抽菸嗎？

●超好用對話

A：It was a great party, Mr. and Mrs. Rose.
B：Thank you, Amy. I hope you enjoyed it.
A：Yes, I did. And meeting new people was fun.
B：Good! Thanks for coming, Amy!
A：Thank you for inviting me.

中譯

A：派對很棒，羅斯先生、羅斯太太。
B：謝謝妳，艾咪，我希望妳玩得很開心。
A：有啊，而且認識新朋友很有趣。
B：那就好！謝謝妳來，艾咪！
A：謝謝你們邀請我。

精選
單字

great	hope	meet	fun
很棒的	希望	遇見，認識	有趣的
party	enjoy	new	invite
派對	享受	新的	邀請

1 ■ It's time to <u>go home</u>.

該是<u>回家</u>的時候了。

It's time to go to school.

■ 該是上學的時候了。

It's time to tell you the truth.

■ 該是告訴你真相的時候了。

替換看看

clean up	go out	say good-bye
清理	出門	說再見
leave	go to bed	go
離開	上床睡覺	走

2 ■ <u>Everything</u> was so nice.

<u>一切</u>都很棒。

He was so kind.

■ 他人真是和善。

It was so cold.

■ 天氣好冷。

替換看看

The food	Everyone	The music
食物	大家	音樂
The cocktail	The host	The cake
雞尾酒	主持人	蛋糕

1 我要這樣說 1-81

- I think I have to go now.

  我想我現在該走了。

- I really enjoyed the party.

  我真的在派對玩得很開心。

- Everything was so nice.

  一切都很棒。

- Dinner was just delicious.

  晚餐真是太好吃了。

- It's been nice talking with you.

  跟你聊天很愉快。

2 你要那樣說

- How about getting you a car?

  幫你叫個車怎麼樣？

- Could I give you a lift?

  我能載你一程嗎？

- We'll see you again.

  我們回頭見。

- Thanks for coming.

  謝謝你來。

- Please come to our house next time.

  下次請來我家玩。

UNIT **1** ★ 我要一房一廳的公寓 ⬤ 2-1

●超好用對話

A：May I help you?

B：Yes, I'm looking for a one-bedroom apartment.

A：What's your budget?

B：Well, five hundred a month.

中譯

A：我可以幫您嗎？
B：是的，麻煩你。我在找一間單房的公寓。
A：您的預算是多少呢？
B：這個嘛，一個月五千元。

help 幫忙	bedroom 臥室	budget 預算	hundred 百
look for 尋找	apartment 公寓	five 五	month 月份

1 超好用句型

1 ■ Is it near the <u>train station</u>?
它離<u>火車站</u>近嗎？

Is it far from here?
■ 它離這裡很遠嗎？

Is it on this street?
■ 它是在這條街上嗎？

替換看看

post office	shopping mall	park
郵局	購物中心	公園
bank	stationary store	drugstore
銀行	文具店	藥局

2 ■ You have to pay <u>the gas</u>.
你必須付<u>瓦斯費</u>。

We have to send a letter.
■ 我們必須去寄信。

You have to leave now.
■ 你必須現在離開。

替換看看

the heat	the electricity	your own electricity
暖氣費	電費	你自己的電費
extra money	a deposit	seven thousand dollars a month
額外的錢	一筆訂金	一個月七千元

★打開話題的好句子

1 我要這樣說

 2-3

■ I'm looking for a one-bedroom apartment.

我在找一間單房的公寓。

■ How much is the rent?

房租多少錢？

■ Is this an elevator?

有電梯嗎？

■ Are utilities included?

有包含公用設備（水電、煤氣）嗎？

■ I'd like a view of the lake.

我希望可以看到湖。

2 你要那樣說

■ I am looking for a part-time job.

我在找一份兼職的工作。

■ Are you hiring?

你們有在徵人嗎？

■ What is the salary?

薪水怎麼算？

■ I have a master's degree.

我有碩士學位。

■ Any work experience?

有工作經驗嗎？

●超好用對話

A：Excuse me. Do you have paper cups?

B：Yes, of course. They're behind the
　　baby products.

A：And where are the baby products?

B：Right there, ma'am.

A：Oh, I see it. Thank you.

■■ 中譯

A：不好意思，你們有（賣）紙杯
　　嗎？
B：當然有。它們在嬰兒用品後面。
A：那麼嬰兒用品在哪裡呢？
B：就在那裡，小姐。
A：噢，我看到了，謝謝你。

精選
單字

excuse me 不好意思	cup 杯子	baby 嬰兒	there 那邊
paper 紙	behind 後面	product 產品	ma'am (尊稱)女士，夫人

1 超好用句型

1 ■ **What aisle is the <u>sugar</u> in?**
糖放在哪一個走道上呢？

What time is she arriving?
■ 她幾點會到呢？

What book are you looking for?
■ 你在找哪一本書呢？

替換看看

shampoo	flour	canned food
洗髮精	麵粉	罐頭
milk	cereal	salt
牛奶	穀片	鹽

2 ■ **Do you have any <u>dish soap</u>?**
你們有洗碗精嗎？

Do you have the directions?
■ 你知道路嗎？

Do you have to leave now?
■ 你們一定要現在離開嗎？

替換看看

cabbage	eggs	coffee
高麗菜	蛋	咖啡
ketchup	chocolate	bananas
番茄醬	巧克力	香蕉

★打開話題的好句子

1 我要這樣說 2-6

- **Excuse me. Where are the onions?**

  不好意思，請問洋蔥放在哪裡？

- **It's at the back.**

  它在後面。

- **I'll ask a shop clerk for you.**

  我幫你問一下店員。

- **Do I line up here?**

  是在這裡排隊嗎？

- **Are you the last in line?**

  你是排隊的最後一個嗎？

2 你要那樣說

- **I can't find the chocolate.**

  我找不到巧克力（在哪裡）。

- **Do you have any dish soap?**

  你們有洗碗精嗎？

- **Can I have an extra bag?**

  可以再多給我一個袋子嗎？

- **I don't need a plastic bag, thank you.**

  我不需要塑膠袋，謝謝你。

- **Can I use a credit card?**

  我可以刷信用卡嗎？

UNIT 3 ★ 流行服飾在幾樓

 2-7

● 超好用對話

A：May I help you?

B：Yes. I'm looking for a T-shirt.

A：How about these?

B：Hmm… Do you have larger ones?

A：Yes, we do. Here they are.

B：Let's see… I like this one.
　　May I try it on?

中譯

A：我可以為您效勞嗎？
B：是的，我在找襯衫。
A：這些怎麼樣？
B：嗯...你們有沒有比較大的襯衫？
A：有的。就是這些。
B：我看看...我喜歡這件。我可以試穿嗎？

精選
單字

help 幫忙	T-shirt T恤	larger 比較大的	this 這個
look for 尋找	these 這些	like 喜歡	try 嘗試 (try on試穿)

1 ■ Is there a <u>department store</u> in this area?
這一帶有<u>百貨公司</u>嗎？

Is there a school near here?
■ 這附近有學校嗎？

Is there a card on the table?
■ 桌上有一張卡片嗎？

替換看看

shopping mall	grocery store	supermarket
購物商場	雜貨店	超級市場
convenience store	sporting goods store	book store
便利商店	運動用品店	書局

2 ■ Where is/are <u>women's wear</u>?
女裝在哪裡？

Where is the entrance?
■ 入口在哪裡？

Where is the fitting room?
■ 試衣間在哪裡？

替換看看

men's wear	children's wear	home appliances
男裝	童裝	家電
the pharmacy	the information desk	the entrance／exit
藥品	服務台	入口／出口

★打開話題的好句子 • • • • • • • • • • •

▄1 我要這樣說

 2-9

- May I help you?

  我可以幫您嗎？

- Where is the toy department?

  玩具部在哪裡？

- I'm looking for men's shoes.

  我在找男用鞋。

- It's on the third floor.

  它在三樓。

- Take the elevator.

  請坐電梯。

▄2 你要那樣說

- That's a real bargain.

  那真是太划算了。

- Is this for men or women?

  這是給男生的還是女生的？

- Can I see this?

  我可看看這個嗎？

- I'm just looking.

  我只是看看。

- Can you giftwrap it for me?

  你可以幫我包裝一下嗎？

●超好用對話

A：Good afternoon, sir. How may I help you?

B：I'd like to cash a check, please.

A：No problem.

B：And I'd also like to make a deposit.

A：Sure. Please fill out this form first.

■■■中譯

A：午安，先生，我該如何為您效勞呢？
B：麻煩你，我想要兌現一張支票。
A：沒問題。
B：我還想要存錢。
A：當然。請先填好這個表格。

精選單字

afternoon 下午	cash 現金，兌現	deposit 存款	form 表格
sir (尊稱) 先生	check 支票	fill 填滿	first 第一，首先

1 超好用句型

1 ■ **I'd like to cash a check.**
我想要兌現一張支票。

I'd like to stay here.
■ 我想要待在這裡。

I'd like to order 3 cups of coffee.
■ 我要點三杯咖啡。

替 換 看 看

make a deposit	transfer money	make a transfer
存錢	轉帳	轉帳
open an account	close my account	apply for a loan
開戶	解約帳戶	申請貸款

2 ■ **How many pounds to the dollar?**
美元兌換英鎊的匯率是多少？

How many days did you stay?
■ 你待了幾天？

How many times have you been there?
■ 你去過那裡多少次了？

替 換 看 看

Francs	Yen	New Taiwan Dollars
法郎	日圓	新台幣
Rupees	Pesos	Euros
盧比	披索	歐元

★打開話題的好句子

. . . .

1 我要這樣說

2-12

- Is there a bank near here?

  這附近有銀行嗎？

- Would you cash these traveler's checks?

  你可以兌現這些旅遊支票嗎？

- With some change, please.

  請給我一些零錢。

- Into ten dollar bills, please.

  麻煩請都換成十塊錢。

- May I see your ID?

  我可以看一下您的身分證嗎？

2 你要那樣說

- I'd like to open a savings account.

  我想要開立一個存款帳戶。

- What's the interest rate?

  利率是多少？

- Are you a customer here?

  您是這裡的顧客嗎？

- Press your PIN number here.

  請在此鍵入您的個人識別號碼。

- You need to fill in that form first.

  您得先把那張表格填妥。

●超好用對話

A：What can I do for you?

B：I need to send a letter by air mail to Japan.

A：Sure, but I need your return address, please.

B：OK. How much is the postage?

A：26 dollars.

中譯

A：我能為您做什麼呢？
B：我要寄一封航空信件到日本。
A：當然，但我需要寄件人地址，麻煩您。
B：好的。郵資多少？
A：二十六塊錢。

精選單字

send 寄送	air mail 航空信件	return 返回	postage 郵資
letter 信件	Japan 日本	address 地址	dollar 元

1 超好用句型

1 ■ I need <u>some stamps</u>, please.
我需要<u>一些郵票</u>，謝謝。

I need another vacation.
■ 我還需要放一次假。

I need a haircut.
■ 我需要剪個頭髮。

替換看看

an envelope	to send a letter	to send a parcel
一個信封	寄一封信	寄一件包裹
a mail-order catalogue	the zip code	your return address
一份郵購產品目錄	郵遞區號	寄件人地址

2 ■ By <u>air mail</u> to Taiwan, please.
寄到台灣的<u>航空信</u>，謝謝。

I go to school by bus.
■ 我搭公車上學。

He practices English by speaking with native speakers.
■ 他和母語人士交談來練習英文。

替換看看

registered mail	express mail	overnight mail
掛號件	特快件	隔夜特快件
surface mail	first-class mail	prompt mail
平信（使用地面運輸工具）	特急件	即時件

★打開話題的好句子 • • • • • • • • • • • • • •

1 我要這樣說

 2-15

- Excuse me, I want to mail this.

  不好意思，我想要寄這個。

- How much is the postage?

  郵資是多少錢？

- Air mail, please.

  航空信，謝謝。

- First class, please.

  特急件，謝謝。

- What's inside?

  裡面裝的是什麼？

2 你要那樣說

- What is the cheapest way to send this?

  寄這個最便宜的方式是什麼？

- Just put this into the mailbox.

  把這個投入郵筒就可以了。

- Can you weigh this?

  你可以秤一下這個的重量嗎？

- How long will it take?

  那會花上多久時間？

- I need some stamps, please.

  我需要一些郵票，謝謝。

●超好用對話

A：Would you like to have dinner?

B：Yes, I am hungry.

A：Me too. I know a good Italian restaurant.

B：That's great. Let's go.

 中譯

A：你想吃晚餐嗎？
B：好啊，我餓了。
A：我也是。我知道一間很棒的義大利餐廳。
B：那太好了，我們走吧。

 精選單字

dinner	know	Italian	great
晚餐 (have dinner 吃晚餐)	知道	義大利的	很棒的
hungry	good	restaurant	let's go
飢餓的	很好的	餐廳	我們走吧

1 超好用句型

1 ■ **Do they have <u>seafood</u>?**
他們有海鮮嗎？

Do you have a dress code?
■ 你們有服儀規定嗎？

Do you have green tea?
■ 你們有綠茶嗎？

替 換 看 看

steak	beef	iced coffee
牛排	牛肉	冰咖啡
broccoli	stew	lamb
花椰菜	燉菜	羊肉

2 ■ **How is the <u>wine list</u>?**
酒類的清單怎麼樣？

How is the weather?
■ 天氣如何？

How is the steak?
■ 牛排怎麼樣？

替 換 看 看

soup	cake	asparagus
湯	蛋糕	蘆筍
pan cake	sausage	appetizer
煎餅	香腸	開胃菜

★打開話題的好句子

2-18

■ Let's have dinner now.

我們現在來吃晚餐吧。

■ Well, what shall we eat?

嗯，我們要吃什麼呢？

■ What would you like to eat?

你想要吃什麼呢？

■ I know a good Italian restaurant.

我知道一間很棒的義大利餐廳。

■ You should try that restaurant.

你應該去那間餐廳試試。

2 你要那樣說

■ The food there is very good.

那裡的餐點很好吃。

■ They also have a variety of cakes.

他們還有很多種類的蛋糕。

■ They use very fresh vegetables.

他們使用的蔬菜非常新鮮。

■ I don't feel like eating pizza now.

我現在不想吃披薩。

■ It's a little expensive, I think.

我覺得它有點貴。

UNIT 7 ★ 終於有位子了

 2-19

●超好用對話

A：Good evening, sir. May I help you?

B：Good evening. I would like a non-smoking table for four.

A：Do you have a reservation, sir?

B：No, we don't have a reservation.

A：Then I'm sorry, sir. I'm afraid you have to wait.

中譯

A：晚安，先生。我可以為您效勞嗎？
B：晚安。我想要一張四個人的非吸菸桌。
A：您有訂位嗎，先生？
B：不，我們沒有預約訂位。
A：那麼我很抱歉，先生，恐怕您必須等一等了。

精選單字

evening	smoking	reservation	afraid
晚上	吸菸	預約訂位	害怕，恐怕

non-	table	then	wait
不是，非…	桌子	那麼，然後	等候

1 超好用句型

1 ■ **I would like a non-smoking table for <u>two</u>.**
我想要非吸菸區的兩個位子。

I would like to try it.
■ 我想試試看這個。

I would like to play with you.
■ 我想和你一起玩。

替 換 看 看

five	six	three
五	六	三
ten	eight	seven
十	八	七

2 ■ **We didn't <u>have a reservation</u>.**
我們沒有（不）訂位。

We didn't go to the show.
■ 我們沒有去看表演。

We didn't talk to him.
■ 我們沒和他交談。

替 換 看 看

buy wine	like the food	know how to eat
買酒	喜歡那些餐點	知道怎麼吃
order dessert	see the price	enjoy the meal
點甜點	看到價錢	吃得很開心

★打開話題的好句子

1 我要這樣說

 2-21

■ Welcome to Joe's!

歡迎來到喬的地盤！

■ Do you have a reservation?

你們有預約訂位嗎？

■ I have a reservation.

我有訂位。

■ How many of you, sir?

你們總共幾位呢，先生？

■ Two, please.

兩位，謝謝。

2 你要那樣說

■ I'm sorry, the tables are full.

我很抱歉，已經客滿了。

■ How long do we have to wait?

我們要等多久呢？

■ Would you like to sit by the window?

請問你們想要坐窗邊的位子嗎？

■ Smoking or non-smoking?

吸菸還是非吸菸區呢？

■ This way, please.

這邊請。

●超好用對話

A：A chicken salad sandwich and a Coke, please.

B：Sure. Is that all?

A：Uh…do you have muffins?

B：Yes, chocolate and banana.

A：Banana, please.

中譯

A：一個雞肉沙拉三明治和可樂。
B：好的。還有什麼嗎？
A：呃...你們有（賣）杯子蛋糕嗎？
B：有的，巧克力和香蕉口味。
A：香蕉，麻煩你。

精選單字

chicken	sandwich	all	chocolate
雞肉	三明治	全部	巧克力

salad	Coke	muffin	banana
沙拉	可樂	杯子蛋糕	香蕉

1 超好用句型

1 ■ Do you have <u>spaghetti</u>?
你有<u>義大利麵</u>嗎？

Do you have a pen?
■ 你有筆嗎？

Do you have a nickname?
■ 你有綽號嗎？

替換看看

hamburgers	beef noodles	pizza
漢堡	牛肉麵	比薩
hot pot	curry rice	Korean BBQ
火鍋	咖哩飯	韓國烤肉

2 ■ <u>This</u> and <u>this</u>, please.
我要<u>這個</u>跟<u>這個</u>。

Tens and twenties, please.
■ 十塊和二十塊，謝謝。

Croissant and milk, please.
■ 可頌麵包和牛奶，謝謝。

替換看看

potatoes／veal	mutton／lobster	prawns／salmon
馬鈴薯／小牛肉	羊肉／龍蝦	大蝦／鮭魚
oysters／sirloin	boiled fish／mixed vegetables	baked chicken／garden salad
生蠔／沙朗牛排	白煮魚／綜合鮮蔬	烤雞／庭園沙拉

★打開話題的好句子

1 我要這樣說

2-24

- **Are you ready to order, sir?**

  您要點餐了嗎，先生？

- **What do you suggest?**

  你推薦什麼（餐點）呢？

- **What is today's special?**

  今日的特餐是？

- **This and this, please.**

  這個和這個，謝謝。

- **I'll have the same, please.**

  我也點一樣的，謝謝。

2 你要那樣說

- **Do you have any local dishes?**

  你們有當地特色餐點嗎？

- **I'd like some vegetables as an appetizer.**

  開胃菜我想要來點蔬菜。

- **I'll have fish as the main dish.**

  我的主菜要魚。

- **Let's try this one.**

  我們來試試這個吧。

- **How would you like your steak?**

  您的牛排要幾分熟？

UNIT 9 ★ 我們各付各的

 2-25

●超好用對話

A：Can I have the check, please?

B：One moment, sir.

A：Oh, and um…separate checks, please.

B：Separate checks? Of course.

A：Thank you.

中譯

A：結帳，麻煩你。
B：稍等一下，先生。
A：噢，還有我們要分開付。
B：分開嗎？當然。
A：謝謝你。

 精選單字

can 可以	please 請	sir (尊稱)先生	of course 當然
check 帳單	moment 片刻	separate 分開的	thank 感謝

1 ■ <u>Go Dutch</u>, please.
分開付,謝謝。

We will pay separately.
■ 我們要分開付帳。

This is my treat.
■ 這次我請客。

替換看看

Charge	Separate checks	Split the bill
結帳	個別付帳	分開付
Be my guest this time	This is on me	Let me foot the bill
這次我請客	這次我請客	讓我出(錢)吧

2 ■ Could I have <u>the bill</u>?
可以給我帳單嗎?

Could we switch seats?
■ 我們可以換位子嗎?

Could you give us some napkins?
■ 你可以給我們一些餐巾紙嗎?

替換看看

the receipt	the check	the menu
收據	帳單	菜單
another fork	a small plate	more bread
另一支叉子	一個小盤子	更多麵包

1 我要這樣說

 2-27

■ Check, please.

付帳，謝謝。

■ Let's go halves.

我們平均分攤吧。

■ Do you accept credit cards?

你們收信用卡嗎？

■ Is it including the service charge?

有包含服務費嗎？

■ Sorry, sir. We don't accept credit cards.

很抱歉，先生，我們不收信用卡。

2 你要那樣說

■ I think I have the wrong change.

我想是找錯錢了。

■ Here's your change and receipt, sir.

這是你的找錢和收據，先生。

■ Keep the change.

不用找了。

■ It's delicious.

東西很好吃。

■ Can we have a doggie bag?

我們可以打包嗎？（回家餵狗）

●超好用對話

A：This is a beautiful hat! I want to buy it.

B：Do you wear hats a lot?

A：Yes, I do.

B：Then buy it. I want to buy one, too.

■中譯

A：這帽子真漂亮！我想把它買下來。

B：你常常戴帽子嗎？

A：是啊。

B：那麼就買吧。我也想買一頂。

beautiful	buy	hat	then
漂亮的	購買	帽子	那麼
want	wear	a lot	too
想要	穿戴	很多；常常	也

1 超好用句型

1 ■ I'm looking for a <u>T-shirt</u>.
我在找T恤。

I'm looking for a gift for my brother.
■ 我在找要送給我哥哥（弟弟）的禮物。

I'm looking for something to match this skirt.
■ 我在找件可以搭配這件裙子的。

替換看看

jacket	dress	polo shirt
夾克	洋裝	運動衫
dress shirt	casual shirt	pullover
襯衫	休閒衫	套衫

2 ■ I want the <u>red</u> ones.
我要紅色的。

I want a car.
■ 我想要一輛車。

I want some popcorn.
■ 我要買一些爆玉米花。

替換看看

yellow	gray	orange	red	pink	white
黃色	灰色	橘色	紅色	粉紅色	白色
black	brown	beige	blue	green	purple
黑色	咖啡色	米黃色	藍色	綠色	紫色

★打開話題的好句子

1 我要這樣說　　　2-30

■ Won't you go shopping with me?

你不和我一起去購物嗎？

■ What are you looking for?

你在找什麼？

■ I'm looking for boots.

我在找靴子。

■ I know a good store.

我知道一間很棒的店。

■ I'm just looking.

我只是隨意看看。

2 你要那樣說

■ Why don't you try it on?

你何不試穿看看？

■ How does it fit?

合身嗎？

■ This is nice!

這很不賴耶！

■ What is this made of?

這是用什麼做的？

■ Is this washable?

這個可以洗嗎？

●超好用對話

A：I'm looking for heels.

B：What size are you looking for?

A：7, please.

B：How about these?

A：Oh, I like this one. How much are these heels?

B：Fifteen dollars.

中譯

A：我在找高跟鞋。
B：您在找什麼樣尺寸的呢？
A：7號，謝謝。
B：那麼這些如何？
A：噢，我喜歡這雙，這雙多少錢？
B：十五塊美金。

精選單字

look for 尋找	size 尺寸	like 喜歡	fifteen 十五
heel 腳跟，鞋跟 (heels 高跟鞋)	please 請	how much 多少(錢)	dollar 元

1 ■ Do you have <u>a larger size</u>?

有<u>大一點的尺寸</u>嗎？

Do you have a bigger one?

■ 有大一點的嗎？

Do you have cheaper ones?

■ 有便宜一點的嗎？

替換看看

a medium	an extra-large	a smaller size
中碼	特大	小一點
an extra small	another color	blue ones
特小	另一個顏色	藍色的

2 ■ How much are these <u>heels</u>?

這雙<u>高跟鞋</u>多少錢？

How much is this large bag?

■ 這個大包包要多少錢？

How much is that computer?

■ 那台電腦要多少錢？

替換看看

sneakers	pumps	dress shoes
帆布運動鞋	氣墊鞋	女用搭配裙子的鞋子
mules	boots	sandals
拖鞋	靴子	涼鞋

★打開話題的好句子

4

1 我要這樣說   2-33

- **This is the right size for you.**

  這的尺寸對你來說剛剛好。

- **You look good in sweaters.**

  你穿毛衣很好看。

- **That's not your style.**

  那種類型不適合你。

- **Red is much better.**

  紅色好看多了。

- **I think I'll take it.**

  我想我就買了它吧。

2 你要那樣說

- **It's too much for me.**

  這對我來說太貴了。

- **Can you give me a discount?**

  可以幫我打個折嗎？

- **Does the price include tax?**

  這個價錢有含稅嗎？

- **I'll pay in cash.**

  我付現金。

- **Do you want this wrapped as a gift?**

  您這個要包成禮物嗎？

●超好用對話

A：I'd like a city map, please.

B：Sure. Are you here on vacation?

A：Yes, I am. But I don't know where to go next. Any suggestions?

B：I think you should visit the National Palace.

A：OK. I hope it's not too far away from here.

中譯

A：我想要一張城市地圖。
B：好的。你是來這裡度假的嗎？
A：是啊，但我不曉得接下來要去哪裡。有什麼建議嗎？
B：我認為你該去一下故宮。
A：好啊。希望那裡沒有離這裡太遠。

精選單字

city	vacation	visit	palace
城市	假期	拜訪	王宮
map	suggestion	national	far
地圖	建議	國家的	遠的

1 超好用句型

1 ■ **I'd like <u>a round-trip ticket</u>.**
我想要一張來回票。

I'd like to see the circus.
■ 我想要去看馬戲團。

I'd like a donut, please.
■ 我想要一個甜甜圈，謝謝。

替換看看

a one-way ticket	a window seat	an aisle seat
一張單程票	一個靠窗的座位	一個靠走道的坐位
a city map	to get a taxi	coupon tickets
一張城市地圖	叫輛計程車	回數券

2 ■ **<u>One-way</u> or <u>round-trip</u>?**
單程票還是來回票？

Tea or coffee?
■ 茶還是咖啡？

Chocolate or vanilla?
■ 巧克力還是香草？

替換看看

Smoking／non-smoking	Aisle／window seat	Local train／express train
吸菸／非吸菸	走道／靠窗座位	普通車／特快車
Airmail／surface mail	Business class／economy class	Today／tomorrow
航空信／平信	商務艙／經濟艙	今天／明天

★打開話題的好句子

1 我要這樣說

2-36

- Please tell me a place of interest.

  請告訴我一個有趣的地方。

- How much time do you have?

  你有多少時間？

- Where have you been?

  你去過哪些地方了？

- You should visit Taipei 101.

  你應該去一趟台北101。

- It's famous for its beautiful scenery.

  它是因為它美麗的風景而聞名。

2 你要那樣說

- I'd like to book a flight.

  我想要訂機票。

- Which night market do you recommend?

  你推薦哪一個夜市呢？

- The National Palace is a must-see in Taipei.

  故宮博物院是台北必去的一個景點。

- Any suggestions?

  有什麼建議嗎？

- Don't forget about the art museum.

  別忘了美術館喔。

UNIT 13 ★ 幫我拍張照

🎧 2-37

●超好用對話

A：This is my first visit to Japan.

B：Where would you like to go?

A：I'd like to visit Kyoto.

B：Kyoto? Why?

A：It's wonderful. It's a very old city, and I'm interested in Japanese history.

B：I see.

＼ 中譯

A：這是我第一次去日本。
B：你想要去哪裡呢？
A：我想要去京都。
B：京都？為什麼？
A：它很棒！它是很古老的城市，而我對日本歷史很有興趣。
B：我了解了。

精選單字

first 第一次	Japan 日本	old 老的，舊的	Japanese 日本的
visit 拜訪	Kyoto 京都	be interested in 對⋯有興趣	history 歷史

1 超好用句型

1 ▪ **It's <u>wonderful</u>.**
那真是<u>太美好</u>了。

It was unforgettable.
▪ 那真是令人難忘。

That was impressive.
▪ 那真是令人印象深刻。

替換看看

amazing	unbelievable	extraordinary
太驚人了	令人難以置信	太出色了
stunning	great	worth the ticket
太令人震驚了	太棒了	值回票價

2 ▪ **How do you like <u>the view</u>?**
你喜歡<u>這景色</u>嗎？

How did you find this place?
▪ 你是怎麼找到這地方的？

How do you know?
▪ 你怎麼知道？

替換看看

the locals	the traditional food	the museum
當地人	傳統食物	博物館
this place	Taiwan	the city
這地方	台灣	這城市

★打開話題的好句子

1 我要這樣說
 2-39

■ I'll show you around town today.

今天我會帶你在鎮上四處看看。

■ Where would you like to go?

你想要去哪裡呢？

■ I'd like to go to the art gallery.

我想要去畫廊。

■ What are you interested in?

你對什麼感興趣呢？

■ I'm interested in Japanese history.

我對日本歷史有興趣。

2 你要那樣說

■ What a wonder view!

好棒的景色啊！

■ Could you take a picture of us?

可以麻煩你幫我們照張相嗎？

■ Say cheese.

笑一個。

■ We need to get back here at six o'clock.

我們得在六點時回到這裡。

■ Are we ready to go?

我們準備好要出發了嗎？

●超好用對話

A：Good morning.

B：Good morning. How can I help you?

A：Three tickets, please. I want a good seat.

B：Here you are.

C：Hurry! The movie is starting.

中譯

A：早安。

B：早安。我能為您做什麼嗎？

A：三張票，謝謝。我要好位子喔。

B：請。

C：快點！電影要開始了。

精選單字

good 好的	three 三	seat 坐位	movie 電影
morning 早上	ticket 票	hurry 趕快	start 開始

1 超好用句型

1 ■ **How many <u>tickets</u> do you need?**
你需要幾張票呢？

How many people are there?
■ 那邊有幾個人？

How many kids do you have?
■ 你有幾個小孩？

替換看看

maps	adult tickets	children's tickets
地圖	成人票	兒童票
one-way tickets	coupons	round-trip tickets
單程票	回數券	來回票

2 ■ **<u>Two adults</u>, please.**
兩個大人，謝謝。

Latte, please.
■ 拿鐵，謝謝。

Hold on, please.
■ 請稍等一下。

替換看看

Three tickets	Four children's tickets	Front seats
三張票	四張兒童票	前排的座位
Center seats	Express train	Two tickets for 'Spider man'
中間的座位	特快車	兩張《蜘蛛人》的票。

129

★打開話題的好句子 · · · · · · · · · ·

▌1 我要這樣說

2-42

■ I'd like to see a puppet show.

我想要去看布偶戲。

■ What time does the show begin?

表演幾點開始呢？

■ Which ticket do you want?

你想要哪一種票？

■ Two C seats, please.

兩張C座位，謝謝。

■ Is there a matinee today?

今天有下午場嗎？

▌2 你要那樣說

■ Do you have any standing room?

還有站票嗎？

■ I'd like two seats for the orchestra.

我要兩個這交響樂團音樂會的座位。

■ Please choose your seats.

請選擇您的座位。

■ May I see the seating chart, please?

可以讓我看一下座位表嗎？

■ I'm sorry. It's sold out.

我很抱歉，票都賣完了。

UNIT 1 ★ 天氣真好

2-43

A：How's the weather outside?

B：It's raining. That's why I'm so wet.

A：Don't you have an umbrella?

B：No, I don't. It was sunny when I left home.

中譯

A：外面的天氣怎麼樣啊？
B：正在下雨。這就是為什麼我會這麼濕。
A：你沒帶雨傘嗎？
B：沒有啊，我出門的時候天氣還很晴朗呢！

精選單字

weather 天氣	rain 下雨	wet 濕濕的	sunny 晴朗的
outside 外面	why 為什麼	umbrella 雨傘	left 離開（leave的過去式）

1 超好用句型

1 ■ **It's <u>hot</u> today.**
今天真是熱。

It is snowy outside.
■ 外面在下雪。

It's too cold today.
■ 今天太冷了。

替 換 看 看

cool	cold	cloudy
涼快	寒冷	多雲
warm	windy	rainy
溫暖	多風	多雨

2 ■ **The weather is <u>good</u>.**
天氣很好。

The weather was great.
■ 當時天氣很棒。

It was sunny.
■ 當時天氣晴朗。

替 換 看 看

nice	clear	mild
很好	很晴朗	很溫和
terrible	unstable	changeable
糟糕	很多變	很變化多端

★打開話題的好句子

  2-45

■ It's a beautiful day, isn't it?

天氣真棒，不是嗎？

■ It's hot, isn't it?

天氣真熱，不是嗎？

■ It'll be fine tomorrow.

明天天氣會很好。

■ It looks like rain, doesn't it?

好像會下雨，是不是？

■ It's getting a little cold.

天氣變得有點涼了。

2 你要那樣說

■ How's the weather there?

那邊的天氣如何？

■ Spring is almost here.

春天快到了。

■ The days are getting longer.

白天越來越長了。

■ It's typhoon season.

這是多颱的季節。

■ It's already winter.

已是冬天了。

UNIT 2 ★ 你又蹺課了

●超好用對話

A：There's a math test tomorrow.

B：Oh, I forgot about it.

A：I'm going to study for it in the library this afternoon. Do you want to join me?

B：That's a good idea. See you then.

中譯

A：明天有數學考試。
B：噢，我忘了這回事了。
A：今天下午我要去圖書館唸書，準備考試，你要一起來嗎？
B：好主意，到時候見了。

精選單字

math	tomorrow	study	afternoon
數學	明天	學習，研讀	下午

test	forgot	library	join
考試	忘記（forget的過去式）	圖書館	加入

1 超好用句型

1 ■ Our <u>math</u> test is tomorrow.
明天我們有<u>數學</u>考試。

Our meeting is today.
■ 今天有會要開。

Our team is in the playoffs.
■ 我們隊打入複賽了。

替換看看

history	music	art
歷史	音樂	藝術
English	science	social sciences
英文	科學	社會學

2 ■ We have <u>an hour for lunch</u>.
我們有（要）<u>一小時可以吃午餐</u>。

We have some old books.
■ 我們有一些舊書。

We have many good friends.
■ 我們有很多好朋友。

替換看看

to keep our hair short	to wear a school uniform	a big test tomorrow
留短髮	穿制服	明天有大考
no school tomorrow	classes from 8 a.m. to 6 p.m.	a good teacher
明天不用上課	從早上八點上課到晚上六點	一個好老師

★打開話題的好句子

1 我要這樣說

 2-48

- I attend classes.

  我有去上課。

- I never cut classes.

  我從不蹺課。

- I have club practice after school.

  我下課後去參加社團活動。

- We have the 6-3-3 educational system.

  我們是6-3-3學制的。

- The school year is from September to July.

  從九月到七月是一個學期。

2 你要那樣說

- How's school?

  上課還好嗎？

- I study 6 subjects a day.

  我一天上六個科目。

- I study at the library.

  我在圖書館唸書。

- I hand in my homework.

  我交作業。

- I eat lunch at the school cafeteria.

  我在學校餐廳吃午餐。

UNIT 3 ★ 我的興趣是作曲

 2-49

●超好用對話

A：Do you like sports, Sam?

B：Yes, and I like basketball the best. How about you, Beth?

A：I like skiing. It's fun.

B：Oh, is it?

A：Yeah, I like winter sports.

中譯

A：你喜歡運動嗎，山姆？
B：喜歡，而且我最喜歡的是籃球。妳呢，貝絲？
A：我喜歡滑雪，那很有趣呢！
B：喔，是嗎？
A：是啊！我喜歡冬季的運動。

 精選單字

like 喜歡	basketball 籃球	skiing 滑雪	yeah 是的
sports 運動	best 最	fun 有趣的	winter 冬季

1 超好用句型

1 ■ My hobby is <u>collecting cards</u>.
我的嗜好是<u>收集卡片</u>。

My hobby is making songs.
■ 我的興趣是創作歌曲。

I like to write my own stories.
■ 我喜歡寫自己的故事。

替 換 看 看

listening to music	singing karaoke	reading
聽音樂	唱卡拉OK	閱讀
watching TV	surfing the Internet	playing video games
看電視	上網	玩電視遊樂器

2 ■ Do you like <u>classical music</u> ?
你喜歡<u>古典樂</u>嗎？

Do you shop online?
■ 你上網購物嗎？

Do you know her?
■ 你認識她嗎？

替 換 看 看

popular music	jazz	rap
流行樂	爵士樂	饒舌
symphonic music	punk music	hip-hop music
交響樂	龐克樂	嘻哈樂

★打開話題的好句子

1 我要這樣說

2-51

- **What are your hobbies?**

  你的興趣是什麼？

- **Do you like jazz?**

  你喜歡爵士樂嗎？

- **I'm interested in Chinese history.**

  我對中國歷史很感興趣。

- **I like romance novels.**

  我喜歡浪漫小說。

- **He is a wonderful actor.**

  他是一個很棒的演員。

2 你要那樣說

- **I enjoy reading comic books.**

  我很喜歡看漫畫書。

- **My favorite movie is *"Titanic"*.**

  我最喜歡的電影是「凱達尼號」。

- **I hardly watch TV.**

  我很少看電視。

- **I'm not into sports.**

  我對運動不感興趣。

- **I like being a business salesperson.**

  我喜歡當一個業務員。

● 超好用對話

A：Did you watch the baseball game on TV last night?

B：Yes, of course.

A：How was it?

B：Very exciting! Chin-Yuen Chen hit a home run. He's my favorite.

A：He's a good player.

中譯

A：你昨天晚上看了電視轉播的棒球比賽了嗎？
B：當然看了啊！
A：賽況如何？
B：很刺激！陳致遠擊出了一支全壘打。
我最喜歡他了。
A：他是個優秀的選手。

 精選單字

watch 觀看	game 比賽，遊戲	hit 打擊	favorite 最喜歡的
baseball 棒球	exciting 刺激的	home run 全壘打	player 選手

1 超好用句型

1 ■ **What's on TV?**
電視在播什麼？

What's on the desk?
■ 書桌上的是什麼？

What's the movie about?
■ 電影的主題是什麼？

替換看看

tonight	the tube	Channel Five
今晚	有線電視	第五台
HBO	the Discovery channel	the National Geographic channel
美國電影台HBO	探索頻道	國家地理頻道

2 ■ **I like action movies.**
我喜歡動作片。

I like Chinese food.
■ 我喜歡中國菜。

I like my brother.
■ 我喜歡我哥哥（弟弟）

替換看看

romance movies	comedies	animated movies
愛情片	喜劇	動畫
mysteries	horror movies	cartoons
懸疑片	恐怖片	卡通

★打開話題的好句子

1 我要這樣說

2-54

- **Do you watch TV a lot?**

  你常看電視嗎？

- **I often watch dramas.**

  我常看連續劇。

- **It's on Channel 74, starting at 9:00 p.m.**

  它在74頻道，晚上9點開始播放。

- **I recommend it.**

  我推薦它。

- **Stop switching channels.**

  不要一直轉台。

2 你要那樣說

- **Let's watch the news.**

  我們來看新聞吧！

- **Do you like American TV shows?**

  你喜歡看美國電視節目嗎？

- **This show is interesting.**

  這個節目很有趣。

- **I just watch news programs.**

  我只看新聞節目。

- **It's waste of time to watch TV.**

  看電視很浪費時間。

●超好用對話

A：You look amazing today, Jane! New skirt?

B：Yes, it is. Miniskirts are in fashion now.

A：Yeah, I've heard.

B：I thought you weren't interested in fashion.

A：Well, I read fashion magazines sometimes.

中譯

A：妳今天很漂亮呢，珍！新裙子嗎？
B：是啊，現在迷你裙正在流行呢。
A：嗯，我聽說了。
B：我以為妳對流行沒興趣呢。
A：這個嘛，我有時候會看時尚雜誌啊！

精選單字

amazing 令人驚喜的	skirt 裙子 (miniskirt 迷你裙)	heard 聽見 (hear的過去式和過去分詞)	be interested in 對…有興趣
new 新的	fashion 流行，時尚	thought 認為，以為 (think的過去式)	magazine 雜誌

1 超好用句型

1 ■ It is in <u>fashion</u>.
它現在是<u>很流行</u>。

It is so cool.
■ 那好酷喔！

This is out of style.
■ 這已經不流行了。

替換看看

a new fashion	up to date	the fad today
新流行	最新的	最新流行的
trendy	out of style	out of date
時髦的	退流行的	過時的

2 ■ I read <u>fashion magazines</u>.
我有看<u>時尚雜誌</u>。

I read newspapers.
■ 我有看報紙。

What kind of magazine do you like to read?
■ 你喜歡看什麼樣的雜誌？

替換看看

Vogue magazine	Trend reports	posts on a fashion blog
Vogue雜誌	潮流報導	時尚部落格上的文章
Marie Claire magazine	MF (music fashion) magazine	Esquire magazine
美麗佳人雜誌	MF雜誌	Esquire雜誌

1 我要這樣說　　2-57

■ That's the latest fashion.

那是最新的流行。

■ I want to look cool.

我希望看起來很酷。

■ I'm fussy about clothing.

我很講究穿著。

■ I love Prada bags.

我喜歡Prada包包。

■ This color will be fashionable this fall.

這個顏色在秋天會很流行。

2 你要那樣說

■ This is out dated.

這已經退流行了。

■ The dress is really loud.

這洋裝太花俏了。

■ I'm not a good dresser.

我不太會穿衣服。

■ I look great in this shirt.

我穿這件襯衫看起來很棒。

■ What color will be in this winter?

哪個顏色在本季的冬天會很流行呢？

●超好用對話

A：This cake looks delicious.

B：I made it, actually.

A：Really? Can I have some?

B：Sure.

A：Umm…what is this?

B：That's mango.

A：Well, it is very sour!

中譯

A：這蛋糕看起來很好吃的樣子。
B：其實這是我做的。
A：真的嗎？我可以吃一點嗎？
B：當然可以啊！
A：我吃吃看…，這是什麼？
B：這是芒果。
A：嗯，這好酸喔！

cake	made	really	mango
蛋糕	製作 (make的過去式)	真的	芒果
delicious	actually	some	sour
美味的	事實上，其實	一些	酸的

146

1 超好用句型

1 ■ Do you like <u>Taiwanese food</u>?
你喜歡台灣食物嗎？

Do you like your job?
■ 你喜歡你的工作嗎？

Do you like music?
■ 你喜歡音樂嗎？

替 換 看 看

Japanese food	Indian food	Chinese food
日式菜	印度菜	中國菜
Korean food	Italian food	French food
韓國菜	義大利菜	法國菜

2 ■ What kind of <u>beer</u> do you have?
你們有什麼啤酒呢？

What kind of dressing do you have?
■ 你們有什麼醬料呢？

What kind of juice do you have?
■ 你們有什麼果汁呢？

替 換 看 看

wine	salad	dessert
酒	沙拉	點心
steak	pizza	sauce
牛排	比薩	醬汁

★打開話題的好句子

■1 我要這樣說

 2-60

- **What's your favorite food?**

  你最喜歡吃什麼食物？

- **This is so yummy!**

  這真好吃！

- **I'll take you to a Chinese restaurant.**

  我會帶你去一家中國餐廳。

- **How's the taste?**

  味道如何？

- **Do you know what it is?**

  你知道這是什麼嗎？

■2 你要那樣說

- **Let's have a drink this evening.**

  今晚我們去喝一杯吧！

- **What do you drink at dinner?**

  你晚餐喝什麼？

- **Scotch on the rocks, please.**

  麻煩蘇格蘭威士忌酒加冰塊。

- **How about beer?**

  要不要來杯啤酒？

- **I had enough.**

  我不喝了。

UNIT 7 ★ 我一定要去那裡玩

 2-61

●超好用對話

A：Have you been to America?

B：No, not yet.

A：Are you planning to visit America?

B：Yes, I may visit my sister this summer.

A：That would be great.

中譯

A：你去過美國嗎？
B：還沒有。
A：你有計畫去美國旅遊嗎？
B：有啊！我準備這個夏天去找我姊姊。
A：那一定會很棒的！

精選單字

America	plan	sisiter	would
美國	計畫	姊妹	將會（will的過去式）

not yet	visit	summer	great
還沒	拜訪	夏季	很棒的

1 超好用句型

1 ■ **I want to <u>go on a hike</u>.**
我想要去<u>健行</u>。

He wants to go home.
■ 他想要回家。

I want to visit China.
■ 我想要去中國大陸。

替 換 看 看

travel	travel all over the world	meet different people
旅行	環遊世界	認識各式各樣的人
take a group tour	learn about your country	try a different style
跟團	瞭解你們的國家	嘗試不同的風格

2 ■ **I'm going to <u>Los Angeles</u> .**
我要去<u>洛杉磯</u>。

I'm going to fix the bicycle.
■ 我要修理這輛腳踏車。

I'm going to rent a convertible.
■ 我要租一部敞篷車。

替 換 看 看

Europe	New York	go camping
歐洲	紐約	露營
bed	play soccer	leave
上床（睡覺）	踢足球	離開

★打開話題的好句子

1 我要這樣說

2-63

- **Have you seen the Grand Canyon?**

  你參觀過大峽谷嗎？

- **Have you been to Italy?**

  你去過義大利嗎？

- **Where did you go last summer?**

  你去年夏天去哪裡？

- **We went to Paris.**

  我們去了巴黎。

- **I was there on vacation.**

  我在那裡度假。

2 你要那樣說

- **It's nice to visit old temples.**

  去參觀古老的寺廟很不錯。

- **It's the best time to see the snow.**

  這是賞雪的最佳時機了。

- **You shouldn't miss it.**

  你絕對不能錯過。

- **You should take a bus tour.**

  你最好搭公車遊覽。

- **Have a nice trip!**

  祝旅途愉快！

●超好用對話

A：What sports are popular in Taiwan?

B：Well, basketball and baseball are very popular.

A：Which do you like better, baseball or basketball?

B：I like basketball better.

A：Are you good at basketball?

B：No. I like watching it on TV.

中譯

A：台灣流行什麼運動啊？
B：這個嘛，籃球和棒球很受歡迎。
A：棒球和籃球，你比較喜歡哪一個？
B：我比較喜歡籃球。
A：你很會打籃球嗎？
B：不，我是喜歡看電視上的籃球賽。

精選單字

sports	basketball	which	or
運動	籃球	哪一個	或是，還是
popular	baseball	better	TV
流行的，受歡迎的	棒球	比較好	電視（television的簡稱）

1 超好用句型

1 ■ I love <u>playing basketball</u>.
我喜歡打籃球。

I love shopping.
■ 我很喜歡購物。

I love cooking.
■ 我很喜歡烹飪。

替 換 看 看

soccer	golf	tennis
足球	高爾夫球	網球
volleyball	softball	dodge ball
排球	壘球	躲避球

2 ■ I am into <u>soccer</u>.
我很迷足球。

I enjoy playing football.
■ 我很喜歡玩美式足球。

I find tennis very interesting.
■ 我發現網球很有趣。

替 換 看 看

fishing	surfing	yoga
釣魚	滑水	做瑜珈
rock climbing	skiing	bowling
攀岩	滑雪	保齡球

★打開話題的好句子

1 我要這樣說 2-66

- What kind of sports do you like?

  你喜歡什麼樣的運動？

- I like swimming.

  我喜歡游泳。

- Do you play golf?

  你打高爾夫球嗎？

- How often do you play?

  你多久打一次？

- I take a jog twice a week.

  我一個星期慢跑兩次。

2 你要那樣說

- Let's go watch a game tonight.

  我們今晚去看比賽吧！

- They won by only 1 point.

  他們只贏一分。

- I am good at sports.

  我很擅長運動。

- I am a sporty girl.

  我是個愛運動的女孩。

- I'm not good at any sports.

  我什麼運動都不好。

UNIT 9 ★ 我家小狗超可愛的喔 2-67

● 超好用對話

A：Do you have a pet?
B：No, we don't. My husband doesn't like animals.
A：Really?
B：Yeah. But I like animals.
A：That's a shame. My wife loves dogs, so we have two dogs. She runs with them every morning.

中譯

A：你們有養寵物嗎？
B：沒有。我老公不喜歡動物。
A：真的嗎？
B：是啊，但我喜歡動物。
A：那太可惜了。我老婆很喜歡狗，所以我們有養兩隻狗。她每天早上都帶著牠們一起去跑步。

精選單字

pet 寵物	animal 動物	love 喜愛	run 跑步
husband 丈夫	a shame 令人可惜的事	dog 狗	morning 早上

155

1 ■ I have a <u>cat</u>.
我有一隻貓。

I have a camera.
■ 我有一台相機。

I have a pencil.
■ 我有一支鉛筆。

替 換 看 看

dog	rabbit	snake
狗	兔子	蛇
goldfish	turtle	puppy
金魚	烏龜	小狗

2 ■ My pet <u>always obeys me</u>.
我的寵物都很聽我的話。

My pets are wonderful.
■ 我的寵物很棒。

My pet dog is my best friend.
■ 我的寵物狗是我最好的朋友。

替 換 看 看

bites everything	likes to sleep on my arm	is a pure-breed
什麼東西都咬	喜歡睡在我手臂上	是純種的
is a cross-breed	likes to be with people	can shake hands
是配種的	喜歡和人相處	會握手

★打開話題的好句子

■1 我要這樣說

2-69

■Do you have any pets?

你有養寵物嗎？

■I have never seen such a lovely pet.

我從沒看過這麼可愛的寵物。

■What's its name?

牠叫什麼名字？

■What kind of food does it eat?

牠吃什麼樣的食物？

■Come here!

過來這裡！

■2 你要那樣說

■I found her on the street.

我在街上找到她的。

■He barks at strangers.

他會對陌生人叫。

■I take it for a walk every day.

我每天都會帶牠去散個步。

■She is part of the family.

她是這家庭的一份子。

■I took him to a vet.

我帶他去看了獸醫。

●超好用對話

A：Do you believe in fortune-telling?
B：No, I don't. But I'm interested in the Zodiac.
A：You're a Virgo, right?
B：Yeah, and Virgos are very hard-working.
A：Don't forget about the picky part.

中譯

A：你相信算命嗎？
B：不，我不相信。不過我對星座很有興趣。
A：你是處女座的，對吧？
B：是啊，而處女座的人都很認真努力。
A：別忘了還很挑剔啊。

精選單字

believe 相信	Zodiac 星座（黃道帶）	right 對的	picky 挑剔的
fortune 命運	Virgo 處女座	hard-working 認真努力	part 部分

1 超好用句型

1 ■ I'm a/an **Gemini**.
我是雙子座。

He is a Virgo.
■ 他是處女座的。

My father is an Aquarius.
■ 我爸爸是水瓶座的。

替換看看

Aries	Taurus	Cancer
白羊座	金牛座	巨蟹座
Leo	Virgo	Libra
獅子座	處女座	天秤座

2 ■ **Pisces** are very **artistic**.
雙魚座非常有藝術氣息。

You are very kind.
■ 你很和善。

Our kids are very intelligent.
■ 我們的小孩非常聰明。

替換看看

Scorpios／elegant	Sagittariuses／active	Capricorns／stubborn
天蠍座／高雅	射手座／活潑	摩羯座／倔強
Aquariuses／responsible	Leos／optimistic	Virgos／picky
水瓶座／負責任	獅子座／樂觀	處女座／吹毛求疵

★打開話題的好句子

■1 我要這樣說

 2-72

- **What's your Zodiac sign?**

  你是什麼星座的呢？

- **Do you believe in fortune-telling?**

  你相信算命嗎？

- **I can read palms a little.**

  我略通手相。

- **You can try red wooden blocks at the temple.**

  你可以去寺廟試試看擲筊。

■2 你要那樣說

- **I am really out of luck!**

  我的運氣真差！

- **Was that bad luck?**

  那個（的意思）是壞運氣嗎？

- **A big nose will bring you a fortune.**

  大鼻子會為你帶來財富。

- **Palm reading is very popular.**

  看手相很流行。

- **I'm interested in the Zodiac.**

  我對星座很感興趣。

UNIT 11 ★ 好有趣的風俗習慣 2-73

● 超好用對話

A：How do you like Taiwan, Robert?

B：I love Taiwan! Your food is great, and your people are kind.

A：I'm glad to hear that!

B：Oh, and I enjoyed celebrating the Moon Festival with you.

A：Great!

＼ ■■中譯

A：你還喜歡台灣嗎，羅伯特？
B：我愛台灣！你們的食物很好吃，而且人民又親切。
A：我很高興聽你這麼說！
B：噢，而且我和你們一起慶祝中秋節很開心。
A：很好！

| food | kind | enjoy | Moon Festival |
| 食物 | 和善的 | 享受 | 中秋節 |

| people | hear | celebrate | with |
| 人 | 聽 | 慶祝 | 和 |

161

2-74

1 ■ What do/did you do for <u>Lantern Festival</u>?
你們元宵節那天都做些什麼呢？

What do you do on Sundays?
■ 你星期天都做什麼呢？

What do you do on your days off?
■ 你放假時都做什麼呢？

替換看看

Valentine's Day	Mother's Day	Christmas
情人節	母親節	聖誕節
Dragon Boat Festival	Moon Festival	your 30th anniversary
端午節	中秋節	你們的三十周年慶

2 ■ Your <u>forests</u> are beautiful.
你們的森林很漂亮。

The scenery was amazing.
■ 景色實在太美了。

The museums are wonderful.
■ 博物館很棒。

替換看看

mountains	buildings	temples
山	建築物	寺廟
gardens	women	lakes
庭院	女性	湖泊

★打開話題的好句子

▓▓1 我要這樣說

 2-75

■ I like rice and noodles.

我喜歡飯還有麵。

■ Soy milk is really good.

豆漿很好喝。

■ Tai-chi is very good for your health.

太極對你的健康非常有益。

■ Kids receive red envelopes from adults on New Year's Eve.

小孩子在除夕夜那天會收到大人給的紅包。

■ We don't dress in black when we go to a wedding.

我們不會穿著黑衣服去參加婚禮。

▓▓2 你要那樣說

■ I stay with my family on New Year's Eve.

除夕夜那天，我和我的家人聚在一起。

■ When is Dragon Boat Festival?

端午節是什麼時候？

■ What do you do for Lantern Festival?

元宵節時你們都會做什麼呢？

■ Chinese holidays are based on the lunar calendar.

中國的節日是依據陰曆而定。

■ Today is Chinese Valentine's Day.

今天是中國情人節（七夕）。

●超好用對話

A：Oh no, I think I lost my passport!

B：Calm down, Julia. Are you sure?

A：Yes! I can't find it! Maybe I left it in the hotel room.

B：Then let's call the hotel right now.

A：Oh, I hope it's there.

🎀🎀中譯

A：喔，不，我想我把護照給弄丟了！
B：冷靜點，茱莉亞。妳確定嗎？
A：我確定！我找不到！也許我把它忘在飯店房間裡了。
B：那麼我們現在就打電話給飯店。
A：噢，我希望是在那裡。

精選單字

lost 遺失，弄丟 (lose的過去式)	passport 護照	find 找到	left 忘了帶，丟下 (leave的過去式)
my 我的	calm down 冷靜	maybe 或許	hotel 飯店

1 超好用句型

1 ■ I lost my <u>passport</u>.
我遺失了<u>我的護照</u>。

I heard it wrong.
■ 我聽錯了。

I knew it.
■ 那我知道。

替 換 看 看

credit card	keys	camera	luggage	flight ticket
信用卡	鑰匙	照相機	行李	飛機票
necklace	watch	glasses	wallet	i-Pod
項鍊	手錶	眼鏡	皮夾	i-Pod

2 ■ I left it <u>on the bus</u>.
我把它忘在<u>公車上</u>了。

I locked myself out of the car.
■ 我把自己鎖在車外了。

I took the train home.
■ 我是搭火車回家的。

替 換 看 看

on the train	on the table	on the taxi
在火車上	在桌上	在計程車裡
in the hotel	in the room 101	at the cashier
在飯店裡	在101房裡	在收銀台上

★打開話題的好句子 · · · · · · · · · · · · · · · · ·

■ 1 我要這樣說

2-78

■ Watch out!

小心！

■ Hold it! Stop!

不要動！停下來！

■ What happened?

發生什麼事了？

■ Shall I call an ambulance?

要不要我叫救護車？

■ Don't worry! It'll be OK.

別擔心，一切都會沒事的。

■ 2 你要那樣說

■ Catch him!

抓住他！

■ Freeze! Calm down!

不要動！冷靜點！

■ I'll call the police!

我打電話叫警察！

■ A theft report, please.

我要通報一則竊案。

■ Don't touch anything!

不要動任何東西！

UNIT **2** ★ **醫生，我發燒了！** 2-79

●超好用對話

A：Mary, you look tired today.

B：Yeah, and I have a headache.

A：Why do you have a headache?

B：Because I drank too much last night.

A：That's too bad.

中譯

A：瑪麗，妳今天看起來很累呢。
B：是啊，而且我頭痛。
A：為什麼妳會頭痛呢？
B：因為我昨天晚上酒喝太多了。
A：那還真是糟糕。

look 看，看起來	today 今天	because 因為	too 太
tired 疲累的	headache 頭痛	drank 喝 (drink的過去式)	bad 壞的，糟糕的

2-80

1 超好用句型

1 ▪ I have <u>a stomachache</u>.
我肚子痛。

My mother has a cold.
▪ 我媽媽感冒了。

His wife had a baby.
▪ 他太太懷孕了。

替換看看

a headache 頭痛	
a runny nose 流鼻涕	

a backache 背痛	a toothache 牙痛	the flu 感冒	a fever 發燒
a cough 咳嗽	a sore throat 喉嚨痛	food poisoning 食物中毒	diarrhea 腹瀉

2 ▪ My <u>head</u> hurt(s).
我頭痛。

My stomach hurts.
▪ 我胃痛。

She rocks!
▪ 她很酷耶！

替換看看

tummy 肚子	foot／feet 腳
back 背	wrist 手腕

ear 耳朵	lower back 下背部	arm 手臂	throat 喉嚨
neck 脖子	knee(s) 膝蓋	leg 腿	thumb 拇指

★打開話題的好句子

■1 我要這樣說

 2-81

- **You look so pale.**

  你的臉色好蒼白。

- **I have a cough.**

  我咳嗽。

- **I feel dizzy.**

  我頭暈。

- **I got hurt.**

  我受傷了。

- **You had better see a doctor.**

  你最好去看個醫生。

■2 你要那樣說

- **Do you feel any discomfort?**

  你有覺得什麼不舒服的嗎？

- **Open your mouth.**

  張開嘴巴。

- **I'll write you a prescription.**

  我給你開一張處方籤。

- **Take this three times daily.**

  一天吃三次。

- **Take this after meals.**

  這個要飯後再服用。

I good 英語　03

美國人都這樣短短說英語（25K+1MP3）

2015年9月　初版

著者 ● 里昂
發行人 ● 林德勝

出版發行 ● 山田社文化事業有限公司
106
臺北市大安區安和路一段112巷17號7樓
TEL　02-2755-7622
FAX　02-2700-1887

劃撥帳號 ● 19867160號　大原文化事業有限公司

總經銷 ● 聯合發行股份有限公司
新北市新店區寶橋路235巷6弄6號2樓
TEL　02-2917-8022
FAX　02-2915-6275

印刷 ● 上鎰數位科技印刷有限公司
法律顧問 ● 林長振法律事務所　林長振律師

書＋MP3 定價 ● **新台幣299元**
ISBN ● 978-986-246-428-1